H
IS FOR
HAWKESBURY

**Hawkesbury Upton
Literature Festival
Anthology
2015**

*Edited by Debbie Young
Festival Founder & Director*

H is for Hawkesbury
Hawkesbury Upton Literature Festival Anthology 2015
Edited by Debbie Young

Published by Hawkesbury Press
www.hawkesburypress.com
Hawkesbury Upton, Gloucestershire, England

Cover image by Sophie E Tallis
Cover design & interior design by Debbie Young

ISBN 978-0993087974
Also available as an ebook

Contents

FOREWORD

What makes a great literary festival? Readers and writers coming together to share their love of books. Not necessarily famous names or highly qualified readers - just those who share the same passion for the written word.

Even better when the festival is held in a cosy, informal setting, welcoming anyone who'd care to join in the fun without having to stump up a fortune for tickets, transport, parking, and all the little costs that quickly up add at litfests that are far from home.

This was the thinking behind the first ever Hawkesbury Upton Literature Festival, which took place on World Book Night, 23rd April 2015, a celebration designed to encourage adults to read for pleasure.

As a longstanding supporter and volunteer distributor of free books for World Book Night, I wanted to set up a fun, informal evening to enable my local community, the village of Hawkesbury Upton, Gloucestershire, to celebrate this special night. A few friends down the pub, I thought, plus one or two of my author, poet and illustrator chums for some informal readings.

Apparently I wasn't the only one who thought this was a good idea, because before I knew it, I had more than 20 authors and poets vying to take part, and a bevy of local volunteers to help me run it.

Packed with non-stop readings and lively discussions, the evening of the festival went far too quickly for me. That's why I decided to publish this anthology of the work read by the authors and poets present, featuring on its cover a specially commissioned picture by local author and illustrator Sophie E Tallis, as a souvenir of the event. The authors, poets and illustrators came along at their own expense and received no fee, but were happy to share their work free of charge with our large and enthusiastic audience.

I was especially thrilled that international bestseller Katie Fforde came to launch the Festival, and that Orna Ross, a bestselling novelist, poet, and founder of the Alliance of Independent Authors (ALLi), came from London to perform her wonderful poem about the joy of learning to read - the perfect segue from this Foreword to the start of the anthology.

I hope reading this anthology will encourage you to sample more of the contributors' work. Buying a book by any of the Festival authors would be a great way to thank them for taking part. Think of it as an alternative form of ticket pricing!

All profits from the sale of this anthology will help fund the next Hawkesbury Upton Literature Festival, now set to be an annual event.

Now over to Orna Ross...

Debbie Young
Festival Founder & Director
www.hulitfest.com

HALO
A poem by Orna Ross

My brother, Conor, used them as they should be used,
the rings. Hoops of grey rubber to throw at numbered
hooks on a board and make the grownups who came to our place

for their daily drink call out. Well done! when one caught on.
To me, the ring was a thing to twirl atop my four-year-old
pointy finger, till it flew. Or an adornment to array

my arm, making of me a Sheba or a Cleopatra, a queen
of places with names like Abyssinia or Timbucktoo. Their
circle of air was an ocean, pregnant with everything.

And the black board where the men used to chalk
the tally was where, up on a barstool, I liked to practise
writing: A. And B. And C. And where, one day, with dust

dancing round a nearby ray of sunlight, I was caught in
the moment I now know will forever hold me rapt:
when meaning came swimming towards me, white

out of black, and set me smiling: Apple! And Ball!
And Cat! Behind, Conor threw a ring and the men
were calling. Yes! Score! Good man yourself! while I

cast off, and lay down in language, braceletted wrists aloft.

A KETTLE OF FISH
A novel by Ali Bacon

It's hardly the distant past, but things were different then. In 2007 only the cool and arty were on MySpace. Facebook was barely a rumour. Life went on, for the most part, in the cliquey huddles of dim school corridors, around the draughty entrances to shopping precincts or, on special occasions, at the corner table in Hot Shots Italian Coffee Bar.

And this was a special occasion. From April we'd been counting down the days. Our last exam, our last sports day and finally, yesterday, our last last-day-of-term. School was officially over. Faye and I were ready for take-off.

Between us on the fake marble table was an entire lipstick collection; not the stub ends from our grubby makeup bags, but a complete new set of testers, the cases still gleaming, the colours ranked in order from palest pink to crimson, each tip chiselled to a sharp edge. I'd borrowed them from Mum's Avon cupboard. She knew I borrowed things and I knew she knew. Back then, that's how it was between us.

Faye was deep in concentration. I watched as her hand hovered, hesitated and dropped with hawk-like precision on number fourteen, Wicked Plum. She picked it up and twisted the end so that its waxy length was revealed. It was a good choice.

"Go for it," I said.

She took out a heart-shaped mirror, drew a careful outline around her top lip and filled it in. Pressing her lips together to set the colour, she gave me an extravagant purple pout.

"What d'ye think?"

"Nice," I said. It was. Dead nice. Dead Faye. "You should wear it. Tomorrow."

"You reckon?"

I nodded. Tomorrow Faye's dad was driving us to a summer camp in the Highlands where we'd be paid to round up kids and keep them out of trouble. We'd be away from home for six whole weeks. And after that, there was uni.

Faye leaned forward, peering at my own mouth. "What's yours?"

Suddenly, Sugar Ice felt like a cop-out. Okay for meeting Faye to celebrate the end of school, but not for the start of the rest of my life. The lipsticks stood erect in their black plastic caddy like rockets on a launch pad. Before I could change my mind, I made a grab for Faye's mirror, and obliterated the pearly pink undercoat with a manic layer of Showstopper Red.

"Get you!" Faye hooted. "Hot or what?"

Behind me, the outside door swished open. Faye, facing the street, gave me a kick under the table. I scooped the lipstick collection into my canvas bag just as Laura Patterson sauntered in. It would have made her day to have spotted me doling out Avon booty when her gang could afford the big brands.

Laura was at the head of a three-girl posse. "Hi, Faye, hi Ailsa!" She swanned past, swinging a carrier bag, its upmarket logo in full view. At the counter she nudged the girl next to her in an exaggerated way. Their heads inclined towards each other. Over the whoosh and gurgle of the milk steamer, the words "Ailsa Robertson" and "saddo" were clearly audible, followed by muffled laughter.

Faye was watching them. She fixed me with a look.

"Pay no attention, Ails. It's time we were out of here."

This scene, this town, this life.

On the street outside, we did a high five then fell silent.

Faye said, "Come back to mine. Help me pack."

I shook my head. "I said I'd get fish for our tea. I'll have to go up to Kingsgate for it."

Faye rolled her eyes. "All right then. I'll let you off. But remember, tomorrow I'm taking you away from all this." And she gave me a push to send me on my way.

I jogged past the string of estate agents and charity shops until I came to the fistful of concrete and glass that was Kingsgate shopping centre. Before I turned inside, I stopped to take in the view. From this corner, where the High Street became East Port and the New Row ran all the way down to the Nethertown, I could see the red triangles of the Forth Bridge poking above the Ferry Hills, and next to them the grey lattice towers of the road bridge. Arthur's Seat and Edinburgh looked only a stone's throw away. In between and out of sight was the sea, or rather the estuary, where the silver links of the Forth emerged from valleys and mudflats to bump up against the choppy grey waters of the North Sea. That's where the fish came from.

When Mum bought fish it came in a plastic tray, wrapped in film, or frozen into an unappetising brick. But when Dad took off and Mum fell ill, I had lived with Gran. Every week, Gran took a plate from her cupboard, a white one with a faded snowflake pattern, and sent me out to the fish van for "two haddock, not too big." The van came from along the coast. The fish, when it was cooked, flaked open like the top of a lacy wave.

Gran preferred herring, but the herring had been stolen by greedy fishermen from other countries. Gran had been stolen too, struck down by a heart attack when I was twelve, but the plate had found its way into the kitchen cupboard at home, where it guarded its fishy inheritance like a seashell keeps its echo of the sea.

On a recent and more crucial shopping mission (new life, new wardrobe), I had spied two additions to the shopping centre. The Dunfermline Deli sounded like a contradiction in terms, but by now even the east of Scotland was experiencing a bit of a gastronomic renaissance. Next to the deli was a real live fishmonger's shop. Catch of the Day, read the sign, then in smaller letters: brought to you by Mackay & Son, purveyors of quality fish and game.

The Mackays had always had a fish shop, and in the days when it was still in the High Street, Gran had taken me there. Not for the fish ("not as fresh as off the van") but to call on her crony, Mrs Mackay. With her pebble-thick specs and chest as big as any man's, Mrs Mackay had scared me half to death. While she asked me how I was getting on at school, she folded her hands across her blue-and-white striped stomach and looked at me as if I were an undersized haddock that she might choose to save or toss back in the water. But old Mrs Mackay was long gone. As I drew level with the shop, I saw that the business had skipped a generation. Inside was her grandson, Ian Mackay, wiping down the counter with a damp cloth, very much alive.

Extract from
VAGABOND SHOES
A travel memoir by Jean Burnett

Vodka and Kalashnikovs

From Zugdidi we began a journey up into the high Caucasus Mountains to the forbidden province of Svaneti - an ill-advised trip at that time. Georgian friends said we might be kidnapped or shot.

'Svanetians dislike outsiders.' My interpreter,Tina, told me not to worry.

'There won't be any problem as long as you don't mind about the toilet facilities.' I knew that meant a hole in the ground at the end of the garden. We had already experienced this on several occasions.

In the city of Kutaisi's bustling market, we joined assorted locals including some sturdy older women dressed in deepest black, their skirts reaching to their ankles, gold teeth flashing in the sunlight.

After a ten hour drive up into the mountains through high passes overlooking turquoise lakes it was growing dark, and we were invited to spend the night in a small village with the family of the most formidable-looking of the old ladies.I considered refusing, but Tina whispered hastily. 'Don't upset them or they'll kill us!'

'I thought you said everything would be all right?' I complained. 'You said you knew them all.' Tina shrugged, 'I do know them but they are strange people!'

We entered an all-female household, except for a small grandson. These are pretty much the norm in Svaneti where vendettas are still carried on with enthusiasm and the graveyards are full of men who died in their thirties and forties. The custom of bride stealing is also alive and well.

One of the old ladies had lost her son who was shot defending the honour of his fourteen year old daughter from a local admirer.

'If they come back again we'll be ready for them,' said the first granny, grim-faced. She signalled to the boy who went to retrieve the family's prize possession. In the living room he waved the Kalashnikov rifle above his head, shouting a few Caucasian war cries. The old ladies applauded and boasted of their deadly aim before urging me to drink more home-made vodka. This was urged on us at every meal, especially breakfast.

'It's the elixir of life!' said granny number two, her face splitting into a huge grin. It was reputed that the Amazons came from Georgia; watching the old ladies with their rifle I was willing to believe this.

'Tell people to come here; we need tourists,' pleaded Father Gyorgy, the local priest. I suggested that more modern plumbing and fewer kalashnikovs might be an inducement. He dismissed this notion. 'The plumbing we can arrange, the gun problem is not as bad as it seems.' I laughed nervously as he promised to take me up to Ushguli, Europe's highest inhabited village, on my next visit; only five more hours on atrocious roads but quite mind-blowing, according to Tina.

This was the very edge of Europe, the crossing place, where West meets East. These people are European but their isolation and ancient culture keep them in a time capsule. As Tina had warned me, mountain people are different.

Extract from
JUST MY DOGGEREL
by Joseph Johnson Fairney
(A poetry collection compiled by
his grandson, William Fairney)
*Written after the death of his son, William Dawson
Fairney, on a bombing mission in Hungary in 1944.
Azrael is the Roman god that separates
the Soul from the Body after death.*

AZRAEL

Azrael called me, called me early,
Strong of arm and stout of heart.
Childhood past and manhood, barely;
Hard it was from life to part.
Azrael called me.

Azrael called me. Murmured daily.
Flushed with life and bright of eye.
Free and joyous, singing gaily:
Did we think or dread to die.
Azrael called me.

Azrael called me. In the springtime.
Life with all its joys unknown.
Vision bright of love's sweet springtime
Dispersed and broken, over blown.
Azrael called me.

Azrael called me. From the duty -
Self-imposed, my country's need.
Love and joy and youth and beauty
To the crown the fates decreed.
Azrael called me.

Azrael called me. Sun and shadow
Wind and water, hum of bees.
Flowering glories of the meadows,
Azrael called me up from these.
Azrael called me.

Azrael called me, Shore and waves -
White sails glinting in the sun.
Rocky headland, crag and cave,
By-passed ere my race begun.
Azrael called me.

Azrael called me, "What is fame,
Love of country, duty's call?"
Lip-laudation - but a name.
From the lips of great and small
Futile praise for our endurance
Smoothly phrased to sing to sleep;
Brightened by blest assurance,
Nought to us or Those who Weep.
Azrael called us.

Extract from the first chapter of
LOVE LETTERS
A novel by Katie Fforde

"So, dear," Eleanora said later, and inevitably, Laura felt, "any plans for your future? Do you want to be a writer?"

"Good God, no!" said Lara and then, realising that perhaps she maybe shouldn't have sounded so horrified, went on: "Sorry, I didn't meant to be so vehement, but I would hate to be a writer. I love to get lost in other people's books, but I really don't want to write one myself."

"Such a relief!" said Eleanora. "I felt I had to ask, but I'm really pleased. Any other plans for gainful employment?"

"Not really." She sighed. "I've hardly had time to think about it, and I've got a couple of months before I'm on the dole. I'm sure to find something."

"You don't sound very sure."

Laura tried to make herself clear. "I'm sure I won't starve - there are always jobs for willing workers - but it's unlikely I'll find anything book related, which I love so much. Not in this town, anyway."

Eleanora narrowed her eyes in thought. "I might have something."

Laura turned to her, not sure if she'd heard properly.

"Have you?"

Eleanora leant in. "Mm, something frightfully exciting."

Laura's little flicker of hope died. She didn't do "frightfully exciting". She wouldn't be right for the job. It would probably involve marketing, or starting a business from scratch - not her sort of thing at all.

"Well, don't you want to hear what it is?" Eleanora demanded through a slice of tomato and feta cheese.

Laura speared a black olive with her fork. "Of course. It's so kind of you to take an interest." She hoped Eleanora wouldn't hear her apathy.

"It it, actually," agreed Eleanora, possibly slightly annoyed by Laura's lukewarm response. "And if it wasn't in my interest as well, I wouldn't bother. Too busy. But what it is, is this!"

At that moment a phalanx of waiters descended on the table, whipping away Greek salad and taramasalata and replacing them with sizzling platters of moussaka, sinister fish dishes and more bottles of wine.

While all this was going on, Laura framed an elegant and polite refusal for whatever Eleanora might be about to suggest. She didn't think anything this brightly coloured parrot of a woman could offer her could possibly be up her street. They were too different as people.

"I want you to set up a literary festival!" Eleanora announced with the assumption that this would be greeted with clapping and shrieks of delight, as if she was a conjuror who had just produced a particularly endearing rabbit. "Well, help set up one, anyway."

Visions of the major festivals - Cheltenham, Hay, Edinburgh, with their phalanx of stars, many of them famous for something quite other than writing books - made her feel weak. "I don't think - "

"But it's not just an ordinary lit fest." Eleanora flapped a heavily ringed hand as if it were boredom that made Laura doubtful. "There's a music festival going on too. It's at my niece's house."

"Oh. Big house," said Laura. For a moment, her wayward imagination was distracted by the notion of a two-bed semi with a literary lion in one room and an *X Factor* entry-level band in another.

"Huge. A monster, millstone round their necks, but lovely, of course. They're trying to make it pay its way so they can keep it. The music festival should make them a bit, but my niece, Fenella, wanted a literary festival too, to make it a bit different."

"I think there is a festival already that combines - "

"Doesn't mean they can't have one too, does it?"

"Of course not. I was just saying - "

"The music side of it is all going fine but they've got noone to take over the literary festival bit. You'd be perfect.

Laura shook her head. She wasn't the right sort of entrepreneurial, feisty woman who could blag big firms into sponsoring huge events for ex-presidents who had written heavily ghosted autobiographies. "I don't think so."

"Why on earth not?"

Why didn't Eleanora - obviously a very bright woman - get it? "Because I've never done anything like that before. I wouldn't know where to start!"

Eleanora took a moment and then lowered her voice and spoke slowly, as if to a bewildered child or a frightened horse. "But sweetie, you have done things like that before! What do you think a bookshop event is? You get the authors there, you get them to speak, you make sure people buy their books. Just the same!"

"But we don't have to make vast amounts of money out of the bookshop events, or hire a venue, or anything!"

"Look, I can tell losing your job has knocked your confidence. It would. But don't turn this down until you've had a proper think about it. Fen said there's some sort of meeting at Somerby - hang on, I'll tell you when it is." Eleanora took a big gulp of her wine and then started burrowing in her handbag, which had a Mary Poppins quality: it was enormous and possibly containted a standard lamp. She produce a Filofax the size of a family Bible and riffled through the pages. "Next week. Two o'clock. At Somerby. Do you know where that is?"

"No," said Laura firmly, although a small part of her wanted to find out. Despite her reservations - and they were strong ones - she felt a flutter of interest. Anything to do with books had that effect on her.

First Chapter of
ECHOES OF JUSTICE
A novel by J J Franklin

The first one was easy.

Jean turned the corner and began the long walk past the row of dark shops, grilled and shuttered against the world, towards the off-licence that spilled its beacon across the gloom.

Caught within the circle of light, she could see him slouched against the wall, drinking from a can while several young men lounged about him.

Moving towards the group, she began the old woman shuffle she'd practised, aware that glances passed between them and they watched her, as she guessed they would.

Inside the off-licence, Jean kept up the masquerade, bending to hide her face from the CCTV and checking that her unruly curls remained tucked under her old gardening hat.

Behind the grill a middle-aged man rose, resigned, putting down his racing paper. 'Yes?'

It was important she remain in character and give him nothing to remember her. Jean hesitated, as if still deciding, before pointing to a half bottle of the cheapest whisky.

He reached for the bottle and plonked it down in front of her. 'Four fifty two,' he said, holding out his hand.

While he sighed with impatience and rested his elbow of the counter, Jean counted out the change as if each penny were her last. When she had the exact amount, she dropped the coins into his hand, waiting as he placed the denominations into the correct sections of the cash register.

Banging shut the register, he picked up the whisky, intent on wrapping it in the fragile pink tissue paper that served as an empty semblance of customer service.

'No.' Jean waved her hand to stop him and indicated that he should pass it to her and he glared at her in disgust as if she had contravened some deeply ingrained customer rule. Jean took the whisky and he turned away, shaking his head.

Taking slow steps towards the door, she stopped to tuck the bottle in a side pocket of her shopping bag, away from where the prepared bottle lay ready in its plain plastic bag. Hearing a rustle, she risked glancing around, but the man was ignoring her and had returned to his paper.

Now came the most terrifying part. Jean moved to the door and took a deep breath, standing for a moment before stepping down and away from the protective pool of light. She sensed their eyes on her. The moment had come.

Jean forced herself to take two steps, before stopping as if to begin an anxious search through her bag. To aid her search, she removed the plastic bag with the whisky, placing it on the wall of a neglected flowerbed where a tired brown twig poked up through the cigarette butts and empty beer cans.

The gang moved behind her as one, thinking they were silent, but she heard them and waited. It was just as she imagined.

'Can we help you, Gran?'

'No. No thank you.' Jean tried to make her voice sound frightened while the fear inside turned to triumph.

'Here let me help you with your bags.' He reached out a hand to pick up the bag.

She made a tentative gesture to take it back from him. 'I can manage.' Jean paused, taking a step backwards to look up into his face, directly into the eyes of one of her son's killers.

Jonathan Bernard James smiled, just as he had done in court when the judge pronounced sentence, but his eyes remained narrowed and suspicious. His mother had spoken up for him, told the judge, she'd tried to do her best, but he had turned into a bully like his father, and she couldn't control him. Jean had felt sorry for the woman. Would she cry when her son was dead?

Satisfied, she looked down and moved from one foot to the other. He would have one last chance of redemption. 'That's for my Albert,' she said, making sure her voice quivered.

'Well, guess what, Gran. Your Albert's going on the wagon.'

He lifted the whisky high and his companions dutifully laughed. Her job done, Jean gave a small cry and hobbled away, pausing only at the corner to turn and watch as Jonathan pulled out the bottle. The discarded bag fluttered across the windswept concrete to join with the other rubbish in the gutter, while Jonathan unscrewed the cap and put it to his lips. He hadn't noticed the broken seal. Jean didn't think he would. Likewise, she guessed he wouldn't share much of his prize with the others.

Extract from
A MONUMENT TO HAWKESBURY:
THE WAY WE WERE (1950-2000)
by The Hawkesbury Writers
(Sam Allen, William Fairney, Liz Howard,
Jenny Harris, Betty Salthouse, Anne Weaver,
Debbie Young and Barry Yuill)

Representing the Hawkesbury Writers at the Hawkesbury Upton Literature Festival, Liz Howard read an extract about the village's two remaining pubs, The Fox Inn and The Beaufort Arms. Here is the part about the one which was the venue for our festival, as pictured on the front cover of this anthology.

The Fox Inn

During the 1950s and early 1960s Charlie Milsom was the landlord of The Fox. He used to keep greyhounds in metal pens against the wall of the skittle alley and train them in the quarry that was part of The Fox land at the back of the pub. Frank Watts and friends would often go with him to race them at Eastville Stadium. He also had chickens, using the old Nissen hut in the corner of the field to keep them in.

John M Bleaken remembers that he or his brother Derek would go up to The Fox every evening to get cider for their Gramps, who lived in The Row. The off-licence area of the pub had a small entrance and hatch that opened onto the alley along the side. Customers could go there to buy alcohol to take home. John, who was aged about eight, would give Charlie the quart bottle to fill. Charlie would always ask "Who's that for then?" "My Gramps." "You're not going to drink it, are you? I'd best put a sticker over it", and he would then proceed to put a sticky tape over the top of the cap. If he was lucky, and Charlie was in a good mood, John might be given a packet of Smith's Crisps that were kept in a big tin just inside the hatch.

There was a large barn outside the pub behind where the bus shelter is now. Double doors opened onto the road and more doors onto the side. Charlie kept his car in there and it is thought that, at some point, Ted Bleaken kept a coach with wooden seats there. It was fairly ramshackle and it was pulled down eventually, probably because it was considered dangerous.

After Charlie left, Bill Mundy took over at The Fox for a short while before moving to Corner Cottage in Back Street with his wife, Grace.

In 1968, Bert and Hilda Hutchinson took over the pub which was then owned by West Country Brewery. Bert was a local man from Dursley and had worked at Rolls Royce, Gloucester Aircraft and Parnall's before going into the brewery business in 1956. It was at Parnall's that he met Hilda who was working in the ambulance room. They were married in 1945 and were together for fifty years.

Their daughter Carol was training to be a teacher in 1968, and, when qualified, worked at Patchway High during the day and as a barmaid during the evening - where beer was 1/10d (less than 10p) a pint. Beer, cider and shorts were the main drinks, with lager coming along as an addition. She, and her husband-to-be, John, have happy memories of The Fox and how, along with the Beaufort Arms, the two pubs were the social centres of the village. There was always a great atmosphere with skittles and darts teams playing regularly during the week. Weekends often ended with singing and dancing in the pub. Frank Deacon would be on the piano, (he was the only person in the pub to take snuff), "Bushy" Chappell drumming on the table, Percy Perks sometimes dancing on the darts mat. Ernie Payne would start singing, and then everyone would join in.

The off-licence area was a good place for teenagers to hide and listen to the "goings on" in the pub. According to John M Bleaken, when Charlie was landlord, there was a gap at the bottom of the glass in the hatch, and they would enjoy listening to Frank playing on the piano and Ernie singing, a favourite being "The Little Red Caboosh Behind the Train". Ernie's mellow voice was recorded for posterity by the BBC and others.

Ernie Payne was a regular at The Fox, and Carol and John remember him always sitting in the same seat, playing dominoes. He drank beer during the week and then cider on Saturday lunchtimes and often brought his bread and cheese lunch in to eat at the pub.

The only food Bert served was snacks such as pork pies and rolls. According to Anne Bleaken, Bert's cheese and onion rolls were the best in the village! After skittles matches, the teams were treated to bread and cheese and a slice of onion. The bread and rolls came from Coates' bakery in Hillesley and the onions from Bert's huge 4lb onions grown in The Fox garden. The onions were cut up and salted and vinegared by Hilda. John Bleaken says that it was Bert who started him off growing onions - but Bert would never reveal the secret of how he got them so big! The garden - or field - was huge and Carol used to keep a pony there. The stable was put on the site of the old Nissen hut that the Home Guard had used as their headquarters. Some time before Bert retired, he bought part of the land from the brewery (then Whitbreads) and built his retirement home on it.

On Show Day the pub would be absolutely packed. Working behind the bar there was not time to go down the cellar to replenish bottles of beer, so the crates were stacked upstairs in the off licence area of the pub. Christmas and New Year were also busy times with families coming back home to Hawkesbury.

When Bert and Hilda first moved into the pub, their living accommodation was downstairs. In the late 1970s, alterations were made that enabled the family to live upstairs. The pub toilets were outside in an open yard. During the alterations, an old well was discovered (under what is now the ladies' toilet). It was unusual because it had vaulting inside the well shaft. Unfortunately before anyone realised, the builders had put all their rubble into the well and it was covered over again. Upstairs was the "Buffs' Room" where the Buffs met every Friday night. It was a large room with a store and one end and had a billiard table (never used for billiards!) in the middle of it. This was also the room where the house auctions were held.

Carol remembers the Beaufort Hunt meeting outside The Fox every April to celebrate the Duke's birthday. The Duke was normally on horseback, as Master of the Hounds, and Bert would go outside with a tray of drinks to pass up to all the riders. In 1982 this was recorded as part of a BBC series with presenter Chris Serle (from *That's Life* fame) taking on different professions. This time he was being butler to the Duke and Duchess!

Following Bert and Hilda's retirement in 1984, the pub underwent major alterations and a large inglenook fireplace was discovered. Neil and Mandy Clarke took over and developed a thriving business, extending the dining area upstairs and often serving ninety covers for Sunday lunch. People came from miles around for Neil's steak and kidney pies, not forgetting the cauliflower in a cheese sauce or his delicious omelettes! When Neil and Mandy left, there were a number of changes in the management of The Fox, which at the present time is owned by Enterprise Inns and is run as an Italian restaurant, Flavours of Italy.

A Selection of Flash Fiction
FOUR VERY SHORT STORIES
by John Holland

A HOT SUMMER'S DAY

"Look at little Demelza playing in the sun. She might burn," says Granddad thoughtfully.

"True," says Grandma, reaching into the kitchen drawer. "I'll get the matches."

I GAVE MY HEART

I gave my heart to the waitress in the cafe. Placed it in the dish that said gratuities. Red and throbbing, it looked incongruous with the small change.

"Thank you," she said, hearing the clink, but without looking.

When I called the next day, it was still in the dish.

She was busy with a skinny cappuccino. Timidly, I said, "I see there's a heart in the gratuities."

"Yes," she said. "The tips are divided at the end of the week. The chef has a sharp knife and a steady hand."

"Still," I said, fishing for compliments, "what a lovely gesture from a generous customer."

"But it will only sustain the six of us for a few days each," she said.

Happily, I thought, I have many more where that came from.

KISS?

"I want to kiss you like man kisses a woman," he said, touching her arm gently.

"No," she said, so that his hand on her arm felt like a small corpse.

"But I know that you like me." "Yes, more than that," she said.

"So why?"

"Well, I am married, eight months pregnant, and, of course, your mother."

"You're always joking," he said.

KATE ADIE IS 69

19/09/14 Kate Adie is 69. Naked, she is beautiful, with firm muscles and taut skin. I ask her to wear something from the war zone. She agrees. There is a tiny scar exactly where you want it to be. "Is there any loss of feeling?" I ask. "Well, you do get hardened," she replies. We laugh. But when she comes it's like a Kalashnikov. "I'll have to go now," I say. "Or I'll get flak." "Here," she says. "Borrow this."

Extract from
BABY, BABY
A novel by Mari Howard

Jenny: 10 June 1988

'Here's looking at you, babe!'

A folded piece of A4, a lecture handout from four years ago, flutters to the floor. And I, leaning down to retrieve it, am overtaken by all the gnawing regret of an old love affair I'd intended Cambridge would help me forget.

The cartoon occupies the bottom third of the page, it's drawn in ball pen, and it's ridiculous: under a dinner table, a pair of bony male knees (below a kilt), equipped with human eyes, regard a pair of shapely female legs, ending in elegant feet in high heeled shoes. Max always liked to do daft things, even as he was also absorbing the scientific information. I can see it now, him passing me the drawing while maintaining that serious expression and looking straight ahead at the slide the lecturer had on the screen.

The lecture - early January, 1984, was by one of my father's contacts from CALTEC. It was held in London, and I took Max as my guest. The subject was Hox genes, the genes which are a toolkit for forming the shapes, the phenotypes, of living creatures. The lecturer was talking about inserting the mouse gene - Pax 6 - which encodes for the 'make an eye' - into a fruit fly, where a leg is meant to form. What forms if you do this should be a compound, insect eye. Not a leg, not a mouse eye.

33

And it does. A compound insect eye. I've since seen pictures. I've seen the real thing.

And now, I've just finished my final exams and am clearing up my undergraduate textbooks and stuffing two weeks' dirty washing into a bag for the launderette, having a peaceful, relaxing day... until I saw that reminder.

Disturbed by the strength of my reaction, breatlessness, heart thumping, anger rising, I can't stay here. Grabbing what books I've sorted, and the washing, I set out. Taking with me Dad's present for my twenty-first last year, a Sony CCD-V90 camcorder. Will try to capture Cambridge, like sunshine in a bottle!

At the market, my eye to the viewfinder, is that Daze? My stepsister? Browsing the market stalls? Small and wiry, so unlike me and Hat, great galloping blondes! Daze should be thousands of miles away in Colombia! Why's she here? Lowering the camera, moving closer, I tap her on the shoulder.

'Hey - Daisy! You're back: was it amazing? Not here just to visit me, are you?'

'Four-eyes - gosh, yeah I was gonna come by your place later...'

'Nearly gone already,' I say, ignoring her use of my insulting school nickname, indicating my bag, and noticing something new about Daze. An aggressive, Celtic-style, red and gold dragon undulates over the bump under her black Tshirt. Her straight, black, well-worn jeans must be fastened under that with a whopping great pin. 'Undergraduate stuff...' I say anyway, 'for sale to the next generation. So, was Colombia...'

She smiles her distinct, crooked smile. 'Yeah, it was. Gold Museum: you should see it. Ancient, weird, amazing stuff.' I'm amazed by her belly. 'So what?' Daze says.

'You're preggers: when did that happen?'

Daze glances downwards. 'So I am,' she says, like she'd never noticed the bulge before.

'And?' I say. I can't simply rudely ask, Who's the father? Or even, Are you in a relationship?

Daze tries to move on.

I reach for her: a person can't just get pregnant and have a baby without telling their family anything.

'Hang on,' I say, hand on her shoulder. 'Nobody knew did they? At home?'

'Jen, you look tired.' Daisy picks my hand off herself. 'Go and sleep off your exams. And when do you stop being the big sister to everyone?' She turns away, picks up an orange.

'I just...' I say, standing between her and the stall.

'Just? Just nothing: my body, my baby, huh?' Her fingers pump the orange like she wants to squeeze it then and there.

'Odd you didn't tell anyone and don't want to talk about it.'

Her eyes blaze: 'Odd that you should care so much.'

And stressed, sleep-deprived, and this morning hungover, after Finals, besides being upset by that concrete reminder of Max, I go further. She's really riled me. 'Daze, you are being mysterious, you know... You've been working at a fertility clinic... Now you're pregnant.'

'Give it a rest, Jen,' she says, flinging the orange back onto the pile on the fruit stall. 'I was going to ask you to film the birth but...'

'I don't mean to imply anything - I'm just concerned for you.'

'No need, I've got my own friends. Even discovered a long lost cousin out there. Lost when Mum ran off - she didn't just deprive me of a mum, she took away a whole half of my family!'

'So Daze, he's not - '

'Jen, did I say a male cousin?'

'Good, okay: not that wise for cousins...' She gives me a look: I deserve it. 'Daze, come over if you like, we'll have a coffee - or a herbal tea - or something?'

'You're such a lady bountiful - ' she says. 'Like Mum. Like your mum.'

So then, I totally lose it: 'Mum took you in and looked after you and brought you up! Is that the thanks she gets?' Both of us forget about the shoppers and the browsers at the stripy-awninged stalls as I shout, 'The thanks I get for being a sister to the new girl on the block?'

'You fucking loved doing it, didn't you?' Daze yells. 'You fucking enjoyed doing your caring act.'

1497
All Hallowes Eve
Blackfriars Priory, Gloucester

The scriptorium stood empty, a stillness in it.

The study carrels, twenty eight in all, lined both sides of the long building. Thick damask curtains, normally pulled across each one to cloister the novices, were drawn back, exposing oak desks, displaying a neat collection of ink wells, pen knives and quills. Leather-bound books and manuscripts lay open, exposing the vellum, like crisp linen, the background to letters and illuminations, waiting to be meticulously crafted. More books and manuscripts were stacked on shelves along the centre of the room. At one end was the Prior's study area, set apart to show pre-eminence. The friars had long since retired from their studies.

A sharp October wind blew through the unglazed windows. The bells of St Peter's Abbey rang out, slow and ponderous. On the third chime, the luminous edge of a passing dark cloud revealed a full moon whose light shone through the windows, casting shards of shadows across the wooden floorboards. The curtains rustled softly.

On the floor, eyes staring upwards at the finely crafted, scissor-braced, oak roof lay a young woman, mouth slightly open, lips tinged with blue. She lay at an awkward angle, her body twisted, her fair hair streaked across her face. The claret and plum-coloured marks appearing on her neck were the only evidence of her violent and disrespectful death.

Maverdine Lane

Emmelina moved with the stealth of a fawn grazing in open fields at dawn. Limb by limb, she edged her way to the outside of the bed so as not to disturb Humphrey. Moving the covers to form a lump beside his heaving hulk, she lowered her left leg till her toes touched the cool, wooden floor. Her sleeping husband made a grunting noise and turned onto his back. Emmelina stiffened. Every muscle in her body tensed. Surely, after drinking several flagons of beer in the Fleece Inn, he would not wake. The Fleece, situated on the opposite side of the street, newly built and packed full of pilgrims visiting the abbey, had become a nightly haunt for Humphrey. Still, she held her breath, closed her eyes and waited until he settled.

Confident he was asleep, she raised herself from the bed and tiptoed across the floorboards to a chair in the corner of the bedroom. Her shoes, a gift from Humphrey, made from the finest Cordovan goat leather and imported by her husband from Spain, had been tucked under the chair and her day clothes were draped across the back. Keeping a watchful eye on Humphrey, she pulled on a shift and still barefooted left the bedroom, closing the door behind her as quietly as she could. She crept down the creaky stairs and made her way to the fore-hall where her husband kept a large wooden chest in which he stored his old documents. He rarely looked in there, which was why she had chosen it to hide her faith garments and the wooden pattens she wore when walking through the streets late at night.

Tying the dark-brown woollen over-garment tightly at her small waist, and securing a leather bag to her belt, she covered her head and shoulders with a scarf made from the same material and slipped her stockinged feet into the pattens. She paused at the bottom of the stairs to make a final check on her sleeping husband. His thunderous snores could be heard all through the house. Satisfied he wouldn't wake from his beer induced torpor before morning, she lifted the metal latch on the heavy wooden door and stepped out into Maverdine Lane. A quick glance, in both directions, confirmed no-one was about. Only then did she make her way towards The Cross, an intersection where East, West, North and South Gate streets converged. Here stood the octagonal shaped High Cross towering above the nearby buildings and higher than any of the many smaller preaching crosses scattered about the city. Elaborately carved, with the statues of Kings John and Edward standing proud and upright in their crocketed niches, it was topped with a spire and was a visible landmark. She looked up at them and crossed herself, from habit more than anything else.

Continuing down East Gate Street, she stopped just before the city gate and ducked into an alleyway. It reeked of stale urine and dog mess. She knew the porter would likely be entertaining his lady friend at this hour, which would make it easier for her to slip past him and out onto the fields, which lay beyond the city's defences. Listening out for the familiar sounds of their raucous love-making, and, hearing them, she walked through the East Gate with a confident stride and over the wooden drawbridge, which spanned the old Roman moat, immediately turning left to trace the outer walls of the city towards Gaudy Green. The evening had turned decidedly wintry. She hurried along in the dark, pulling her scarf across her mouth in response to the burning sensation at the back of her throat from the searing cold air.

Now almost a mile from the city she heard the bells of St Peter's Abbey chime twice. On the third chime, the clouds thinned and a full moon illuminated her way. In the stillness of the night, the only other sound to be heard was the swishing of her skirts and the occasional screech of an owl as she made her way upwards to Robin Hoodes Hill. Emmelina strode along the worn footpaths leading her to higher ground. With each step she became more alive, more invigorated. She thought of her fat lump of a husband lying in his drunken stupor and in that moment, a stronger resolve rose within her to carry her along what had now become a steep and thickly forested hill.

Since giving birth to a stillborn daughter three years ago a sombre change had occurred within her. At the same time a hidden facet of her character had emerged. The part that had no feeling and no thought of consequences. It was a cold inner core she retreated to, each and every time Humphrey violated her. When he forced himself upon her she would lay there with her eyes tightly shut and her head turned away from him, listening to his laboured breathing, smelling his sour skin and feeling the touch of his sweaty flesh. Worst of all, was the feel of him inside her, thrusting without tenderness into the delicate parts of her she had not given him permission to enter. She always lay without movement waiting for him to finish so she could turn over and pretend to be asleep. It was at these most vulnerable times she would tell herself, over and over, that one day she would be free of him. She said it to her true self, not the cold shell she became when lying with Humphrey.

During the first few months of living under Humphrey's roof she had made every attempt to stop him but soon realised it was hopeless. He was bigger and stronger and it only hurt her more. The only consolation was the act itself lasted but a few minutes. She longed to be free of the burden of her marriage but she could see no way out. Her secret faith had carried her through the last four years, since her parents had died and given her an outlet, beyond the confines of the home she shared with Humphrey.

As she reached the summit, the trees thinned out until eventually she came upon a clearing in the undergrowth where her fellow followers stood in a circle wearing the habitual dark robes, their bare feet on the cold dark earth. She rummaged in her leather bag and brought out a candle, which she lit from a bank of candles arranged on a makeshift altar on the ground, then took her place. Surrounded by a circle of oneness, of understanding and trust and of knowingness, Emmelina breathed in deeply and closed her eyes. The essence of calm and belonging enveloped her, warming her deadened heart. This was the one time Emmelina was true to herself, her authentic self.

A deep, male voice addressed her as she took her place in the circle.

'Welcome, Saoirse.'

She recognised his voice. It was Finn, his bleached, white hair standing out in the dark night. He looked younger than his years, the kindness in his eyes twinkling in the moonlight.

'Let us begin.'

"How many messages have you had?"

This from Dorian Cook to David Brereton – the boy so watchful and slippery, now a man eroded by friction. The three old friends (if that was what they were) convened in a council of shame, gathered around a dirty-white plastic kitchen table: Dennis Mountford - lumpen and malformed in an offensive maroon sweater, chain-chewing stick after stick after stick of gum, never discarding an old lump, just refreshing it with a new strip; Dorian Cook - unstylishly nearly-bald, palms cupped around a mug of tepid tea, less and less convinced that he was only here out of curiosity; and a taller, tauter, scruffier David Brereton, who appeared to have provided most of the bodyweight now being carried by Mountford. Brereton had retained his hair and those backlit eyes still sparkled with mischief, but his skin was callow and gauzy, stretched cellophane-tight against a jutting skeleton, as if eager to shear off and slide away.

"Five or six..." Eerily, the timbre of Brereton's voice tallied precisely with the version in Cook's memory, barely shifted in pitch. "It's some weirdo who thinks he knows what happened. Winding us up."

Finally out of gum, Mountford was now dismantling the cardboard casing of the packet. He looked from Brereton to Cook, transferring the dismissal, inviting it to be exposed as false confidence. "I don't think so."

"What is it then, Den?" snapped Brereton. "Who exactly is going to bother with this shit after so long?"

Cook fixed his gaze on Mountford. "Maybe that's all it is - a reminder. Someone making sure it isn't forgotten. I can't see what they can do about it all now, though."

"Dorian..." Mountford was twisting panels of cardboard into gnarled little rods and then coiling them together. "I've had messages signed with a 'D'."

Brereton laughed - constricted, asthmatic. "It isn't you, is it, Dor?"

"You know who it fucking is!" Mountford seemed close to collapse. Cook was shocked at the contrast between the younger, bolder child-man and the cowed animal now before him. Brereton rose to his feet and shuffled to the far side of the kitchen, lighting a cigarette to break up the journey. "Beer?"

Cook and Mountford shook their heads. Brereton slid a can of something out of a squat little fridge and settled back at the table. He slurped at the drink and drew elaborately on his cigarette, piping smoke out through his nostrils.

"Dave, I've got to ask..." said Cook, cautiously. "What have you been up to?"

Brereton flashed him a look, and for a moment, Cook caught something familiar – an ambiguity between anger and suspicion.

"I work in a hotel kitchen, Dor. Sous-chef. I'm not the boss but I sometimes get to be the boss. It's the best way – you don't get blamed when things go wrong, but you can claim a bit of glory when they go right."

He grinned and gulped back a lungful of smoke. With every toke, he tapped off non-existent ash into the air and rolled the filter side to side between thumb and forefinger. Cook wondered if Mountford could also sense the confected bravado in these tics and twitches.

"You're both married, aren't ya? I had a couple of goes at that."

Mountford scooped up the chewing-gum sculpture and plunged it into an overflowing pedal-bin. "Look. Never mind what we've been 'up to' in the past. What are we going to do now?"

"We should report it," insisted Cook. "No need for all the details on who we think it might be or why or whatever. Just make it clear that we've been receiving threatening messages and we'd like to know what our options are."

Brereton shook his head. "What are they going to do about it? Shut down the fucking internet?"

"We need to make an official complaint!" insisted Mountford.

Brereton mashed his cigarette into an ashtray and posted it into the empty beer-can. "Thank fuck we've got a legal expert on the case!"

"Well, what do you suggest?" The corners of Mountford's eyes were glinting with tears. "Solve it with sarcasm? I've got kids, David! So does Dorian! These messages aren't some 'weirdo' trying to wind us up. Someone wants to hurt us!"

Brereton crushed the can, tossed it towards a small recycle bin, missed. He smiled, raised both hands - palms out - up in front of his face, and extended all the fingers, wiggling

them around for mock-spooky effect. "Someone. Or something!"

Extract from
SHARON WRIGHT: BUTTERFLY
A novel by John Lynch

In this extract Sharon's husband, a young man known as Buggy who has never before been out of England, has been sent to France by gang boss Cameron to recruit a hit man called Carver. A defrocked policeman called Mitchell is to make the introduction.

After a beer at a table in the hotel's front garden, Mitchell and Buggy strolled through the town towards the Yonne and its quayside. The streets were narrow and the pavements wide enough for only one person at a time. The sun shone on honeyed grey stone.

'When will we see Carver?' Buggy asked.

'We'll look for him tomorrow.'

'Look for him? You don't know where he is?'

'I know he lives here. I know an Englishman in a town like this won't have gone unnoticed. Especially an Englishman as peculiar as Carver.'

After they had passed the cathedral they came to an open square with a great church to the east and the quayside opposite. A large fountain stood in the cobbled square, and tables with sun umbrellas were arranged outside a restaurant. Mitchell took a seat at one of the tables and motioned Buggy to do the same.

'What did you mean,' Buggy said, 'about Carver being peculiar?'

Mitchell stared across the table. 'You're right. The man kills people for a living. Nothing strange about that. Just your loveable English eccentric.'

'I'll tell you what I don't understand,' said Buggy.

'We're only here for a couple of days. I'm not sure we have time for all the things you don't understand.'

'Very funny. When Cameron wanted someone killed, he asked me to find someone and I got Doyle for him.'

Mitchell's response was explosive. 'Will you keep your mouth shut! And what are you telling me for? I don't want to know what you've been up to for Cameron.'

Buggy, beetroot-red, stared away from the table. He fumbled for his cigarettes.

'Don't go huffy on me, Buggy. You can't be tight-lipped and smoke at the same time. It's a physiological impossibility.' Mitchell leaned forward. 'You were going to say, why did Cameron need you to find a killer if he knew Carver. Right?'

Still peeved, Buggy nodded.

'Cameron doesn't know Carver, Buggy. All right? When Cameron decided he wasn't happy about your man, he asked me for help. I'm the one who knows Carver. OK? Carver has his regular clients and he won't work for just anyone. It's one of his rules. He's a big rules man, is Carver.'

The waiter arrived to take their order. Mitchell waved him away. 'Deux minutes, monsieur.'

'There's something else you need to know, Buggy. Carver and I go back a long way. I did him a service when I was in the Job. I kept him out of trouble. So Carver owes me, and Carver won't forget. See, Carver isn't your usual poxy little chancer. When Carver's your friend, you need no other. Loyal to the end, our boy. And when he's your enemy...well, Buggy, just don't let that happen to you. Know what I mean? If you upset Carver, Carver will do you. And I won't stop him.

'One last thing. I'm here to introduce you. Nothing else. As far as he's concerned, I don't know what you want him to do. When you ask him, you make sure I'm not around. Understand?'

Mitchell looked up suddenly. His forefinger, which had been jabbing vigorously at Buggy's chest, was arrested in mid-air. Buggy turned to follow his gaze and saw a man a shade over six feet resting a bike against the stone rim of the fountain. The most striking thing about the man was his eyes. Buggy had never seen green eyes before, but this man's eyes were green. And they were fixed unblinkingly on Mitchell.

Without haste, the newcomer advanced across the cobbles. 'Mitch,' he said. His voice was soft and wellmodulated. 'Is this coincidence? Or are you looking for me?'

Extract from Chapter 2 of

BACK TO THE BLACK AND HOW TO STAY THERE

A self-help guide to effective personal financial management

by Michael MacMahon

MIND OVER MATTER

How to reduce the stress caused by debt

Before we get on to the practical issues surrounding dealing with debt, there is a vitally important aspect of indebtedness: the importance of mindset, or mental attitude.

Being in debt increases stress: that's obvious to everyone who has been in that situation. How we react to that stress greatly influences our success or otherwise in getting out of debt. Sometimes we seek external aids; we might drink more than we usually do, as I did. If we are smokers then we might smoke more, or if we are ex-smokers we might start again, as I did. Increased drug use of all kinds can be related to debt. However, the stress relief we might get from these is only temporary, and costs money, which is not what we want. There is a better and more long-lasting way to manage stress, which is to use our knowledge of how our minds and brains work.

Napoleon Hill, an early writer on the habits and characteristics of successful people, wrote, "In my youth, when I worked as a bank clerk, (this was back in the early 20th century, when credit was hard to come by) I could tell, before a man was 10 feet inside the bank door, whether he expected to get his cheque cashed."

What he didn't say was that less-confident customers probably had their accounts scrutinised more closely before being given any cash. Thus being confident, or at least appearing to be confident, might have helped some of his customers to get cash or, in effect, to get credit despite their accounts not being "in the black".

"That's all very well," I hear you say; "getting credit has not been my problem. That's been easy; now I need to get out of the hole that easy credit got me into." My contention, however, is that exactly the same principle applies here. On my wall is a slogan: "Act as if ..." and it has served me well over the years whenever I was in a difficult situation. It's a very adaptable, multipurpose slogan, meaning that if you act as if things are going well, or are about to go well, then you increase the chances that they will. Let's call it the power of positive expectations.

You might well say that confidence, or maybe overconfidence, or excessively positive expectations, led you to the debt problem you have now. That may or may not be true but your prospects of getting out of this situation are greatly increased if you can manage to remain positive.

My daughters used to laugh about the fact that I always seemed to find a parking space, because I always believed I would (nowadays I don't run a car, so I don't need a parking space). My explanation was that because I believed I'd find one, I was relaxed about it, thus when a space became free I'd see it quickly. It's said that if you are stressed (even about something relatively trivial, such as a parking space) part of your brain shuts down; it's part of the so-called "fight or flight" reflex.

There is a more scientific demonstration of the power of positive expectations, which is sometimes called "The Harvard Experiment" because, although it was carried out in California, it was devised by a Harvard academic, Robert Rosenthal.

The power of positive expectations

The Harvard Experiment demonstrates the value of positive expectations; of ourselves and of others.

This is because our interactions with others reflect our beliefs about ourselves; other people, if they are perceptive, pick up quickly what we think of ourselves and what we expect to happen. Surprising as it seemed when I first heard this theory, they will often try to behave consistently with what they perceive our expectations of them to be.

There is other evidence of this so-called "expectations theory" in the psychology literature: the serious as well as the more popular versions. In case that kind of stuff is not your favourite bedtime reading, this summary of the Harvard Experiment is practical proof: something which sets an example that should be (but is not) followed in every school in the world.

Dr Rosenthal conducted the experiment in 1968, in a school in the San Francisco Bay area. His theory was that children could become brighter when expected to by their teachers and he conducted a study to test the theory. All of the children in the study were administered a nonverbal test of intelligence, disguised as a test that would predict intellectual "blooming."

There were 18 classrooms in the school, three at each of the six grade levels. Within each grade level, the three classrooms were composed of children with above-average ability, average ability, and below-average ability, respectively.

Within each of the 18 classrooms, approximately 20% of the children were chosen at random to form the experimental group. The teachers of these children were told that their pupils' scores on the "Test of Inflected Acquisition" indicated they would show surprising gains in intellectual competence during the next eight months of school. The only difference between the experimental groups and the remainder was in the minds of the teachers.

At the end of the school year all the children were retested with the same test of intelligence. Overall, the children from whom the teachers had been led to expect greater intellectual gain showed a significantly greater gain than did the children in the control group. (If you want more info, you can do a search under Rosenthal & Jacobson, 1968).

Rosenthal's work showed that having high expectations of others can influence their performance in a positive way and to a significant degree.

However there is one further point worthy of repetition. The only difference between the experimental group and the remainder was in the minds of the teachers. That "experimental group" of students, as Rosenthal calls them, was chosen at random. When this fact was revealed to the teachers at the end of the experiment, they were amazed because not only were the measurable results better, but they also reported other benefits, e.g. "behaviour was better; no disciplinary problems; it was a pleasure to teach!" The teachers then assumed that the remarkable results were because of their previously-known teaching performance. "No doubt," said the principal, "but you were chosen at random too."

Extract from the opening of
OYSTER: A BOY WITH POTENTIAL
A short story by Rosalind Minett

I think I once killed a man and I don't know why.

It was four years ago this very day.

The bloke lay at my feet, dead. I don't think I knew him but I couldn't look at his dead face and they didn't make me.

They took him away on a stretcher. I remember that bit. Poking out under the sheet were his shoes with the black stud soles. I never had seen those shoes before, that's for sure. His hands, thin hairs on the back, veiny, grey stuff in the nails, I might've seen them. I always look at hands first.

Some time later, someone came to see me. I was reading Goosebumps, 'A Shiver in your Shoes'. It was for homework. The grey raincoat man came with one of the carers. She smiled at me and sat on my bed to let me know it was all right to speak to him.

The man stared down at me, his chunky hands on my bedrail. 'Jake, I'm a policeman. I need to ask you some questions.'

My eyes were on my book. The two boys were just escaping from the gloomy cave on the remote island....

'You were in the church today.'

... when they heard a ghostly sound. Suddenly....

'Weren't you?'

'Uh.'

'Weren't you, Jake?'

'I'm doing my homework.'

The carer said, 'He's ten, go easy.'

'Ten? He looks a lot more. You're a large lad, Jake. And you were in the church today.'

'Yes. I'm a choirboy.' I closed my book grumpily. I wouldn't enjoy it nearly as much later. I kept my eyes fixed on its cover.

The policeman said loudly. 'A man died, Jake.'

I said, 'I just found him like that.'

He went on talking, asking. He had a moustache. He was a detective. I got fed up saying I didn't remember finding that body, just it being there.

The man looked at my face. 'What's that round your mouth?'

I wiped at it. 'Dunno. Chocolate? I had a bit just now.'

'When? In the church?'

'No. When I was running.'

'When you were running.'

'Yes. No. I can't remember.'

'Why were you running?'

'Just was. Dunno.'

'It's funny you can't remember anything but your carers told me you're the cleverest boy in the Home. So, how long had you been in the church when you saw the man?'

'Dunno. Just sort of noticed him.'

'That's not good enough. You're not helping me.'

I stared and stared at my book cover. 'I've got Goosebumps.'

'Have you now?' The detective stepped forward but the carer said it was enough and took him away. So then I finished my story. The two boys rescued someone and

escaped from the cave and got rewarded. Stupid. That'd
never happen. They'd just get a roasting.

Extract from
AS I WALKED OUT THROUGH SPAIN
IN SEARCH OF LAURIE LEE
A travel memoir by P D Murphy

I sit high above the bay of Vigo on a June day in 2012. It is just after dawn. It is quiet and cool and there is little activity on the water below me. This is the beginning of a journey that will take me 600 miles and across three mountain ranges, from the misty hills of Galicia to the sun-drenched Mediterranean.

My pale fingers stray across the hard contours of a shell, tracing the fluted pattern of ridges; I can detect still the elusive trace of the Atlantic Ocean on its porcelain skin. The scallop shell: the symbol of Saint James carried by pilgrims en route to Santiago de Compostela. When it was alive it would have had over a hundred reflective eyes, assembled around its circumference like a string of rosary beads.

I imagine Laurie Lee sitting in this same spot nearly 80 years ago, high above the crashing waves, looking down on the town of Vigo enveloped by a fine Galician mist. His fingers, hardened and calloused from the London building site and the strings of his fiddle, caressing the feminine pinkfleshed shell, dreaming of loves left behind in England and looking ahead to walking down a long, dusty road all the way to the Mediterranean sea.

For Laurie Lee it was a momentous coming-of-age adventure: "As I left home that morning and walked away from the sleeping village, it never occurred to me that others had done this before."

I have realised, as I have grown older, that every new stage of life feels new and uncharted and as I set out on my quest I, too, am sure that nobody has done this before. I want to feel what Lee felt and, if I am honest, I want some of his magic to rub off on me as I walk out in search of that dusty road shaded by groves of orange trees that Lee dreamed of seeing.

Like a solitary monk praying, my fingers trace their way along the inlets of the shell; a shell that perhaps clung, wideeyed, onto an offshore rock back in 1935 and brought all one hundred of its eyes to bear on the panorama of that moment of arrival.

In 1935 the Royal Mail Line steamer picked its way through the islands in its approach to Vigo. Its black hull snaked through the blue Atlantic waters, its trademark bright yellow twin funnels standing out against the white clouds. The ship was en route to Buenos Aires and had started its journey in Tilbury, London, where Laurie Lee boarded – a £4 one-way ticket in his hand – his savings from a year's labouring.

As the ship docked at Vigo, Lee recorded in his diary: "Out of the unconscious rocking of sea and sleep I was simultaneously woken and hooked to the coast of Spain by the rattling anchor going over the side."

I see, in my mind's eye, a fair-haired, tall, pale-skinned, slim young man step off the boat carrying a knapsack, a blanket and a fiddle. He looks around at the sight of the first foreign town he has set foot in. It is a gentle introduction to a harsh and alien landscape. The soft green hills above the port, so reminiscent to him of the Malverns, shade him from the fierce Spanish sun. The early morning mist rising from the Galician Rías – an intricate network of deep fjords – envelops him in a misleadingly cool cocoon of comfort. He stretches his coltish young limbs, cramped from two days on board. His first faltering steps on his journey across Spain are those of sea legs on dry land.

In the wake of the liner whirlpools of white frothy emotions are strewn all the way back to London and beyond: Betty and Molly (Marquita) Smart, sisters from the Slad Valley, both smitten by Laurie and wracked with pain and longing; Rita Louise, who turned down Laurie's plea to accompany him to Spain; 16-year-old Cleo, daughter of a communist agitator; Mollie, whose gymslip-clad sea-wet body kept him warm on Bognor Regis sands. Laurie Lee was on the run: "I was learning how much easier it was to leave than to stay behind and love."

His thoughts turn to Sophia Rogers – "Sufi" – an exotic Argentinian who had moved to Slad from Buenos Aires. Sufi had taught him the few words of Spanish he knew, including what he prized as the most important, given his imagined journey down through the sun-scorched desert plains of Spain: "¿Un vaso de agua, por favor?" (A glass of water please).

It was his dream to walk down through Spain to Moorish Andalusia and the tip of Africa. Now, as he stands beneath the green Galician hills, he is more likely to be serenaded by the plaintive whirling tones of the Gaita (the traditional

Galician bagpipes) than the duende (the magical spirit) of the flamenco gypsy guitar of southern Andalusia.

He looks up at me, high above him on the hill, and for a moment, as our gaze meets, I see a hint of panic. He is alone, wondering perhaps whether he should have listened to those siren calls of fair English girls, begging him to stay at home or take them with him. He is looking at me, but thinking of his mother and the last time he saw her as he left Slad a year earlier: "The stooping figure of my mother, waist-deep in the grass and caught there like a piece of sheep's wool."

Few with a choice find their way to this part of town. Its population is mostly made up of people from the poorest rungs of society. Many are immigrants escaping persecution, or the dispossessed in search of a better life. A kaleidoscope of people from all over the world squashed into a densely populated few miles or so of land.

In any other circumstances I'd have loved the oriental smells of spice, the shops selling strange fruits, the colours of people from all over the world, often still dressed in the style of their home country. But now I knew that Ellie would be at the peak of her grief and at high risk from anyone with unsound motives.

The road was mostly blocks of flats dating from the fifties. They were grey and very run down. The whole place was made of concrete in some form or other. It wouldn't be attractive at the best of times but in the grey murky light of an overcast day it looked grim.

We walked around for a while asking people if they'd seen Ellie, showing them her photo. It began to get dark and we had no luck. Then I had the idea of asking in a shop. We found one, bought some chocolate and asked the shopkeeper. "If she's run away she may have found her way to Dark Street." The shopkeeper counted out the pennies into the till then pushed the drawer closed. "You can buy anything there, knocked off designer stuff. Drugs. Women. You name it."

I felt the hairs on the back of my neck bristle with fear. "Can you tell us how to get there?"

He must have seen the desperation and determination in our eyes, because he carried on, "See that zebra crossing?"

Our gaze followed the shopkeeper's pointing finger. "Yes."

"You go along that alleyway between the tattoo artists and the bookies. That leads to a block of flats. If you go straight along there you'll see the garages and the lorry park beyond. That's the only place I can suggest."

"Thanks," we said and headed off in that direction. The area was run down. Children played football outside. A dishevelled man sat in a porch, clothes in tatters skin engrained with dirt. "Spare a penny?" he asked. We gave him a chocolate bar, unsure how he'd spend any money.

Posters announcing music nights and rough graffiti emblazoned the walls, swear words and political statements were everywhere, not the elegant wall art of some towns. Old chip papers and tin cans blew around in the wind.

A football kicked by me with such force that I could feel the wind whistling around my legs. It missed me by centimetres and almost tripped me up. I wondered if it had been done on purpose and looked at my would-be assailant, a young boy aged about eight or nine, in a blue tracksuit with holes in the knees and a grubby face. I caught his gaze as the ball passed. We must have stood out in such a depressed area where people suffer from generations of poverty and low expectations.

"That young boy should be indoors," I grumbled. "It's too late for him to be out. Some parents let their youngsters play out all day and it's not good enough. It's as if their parents are glad to see the back of them."

"Play out all day? Play out all day?" Gus stopped and looked straight at me, delight suddenly filling his face. "You might have just solved our problem. This wee lad, if he's out playing football all day might have seen her."

"Brilliant!" I pulled away from Gus and walked over to the youngster.

The boy looked surprised that we were approaching him, but he looked a plucky sort and stood waiting for us to get close to him.

"We're looking for this girl," Gus asked him, tapping the phone to bring up the picture. "Have you seen her?"

"Wots it to you, mister?" he answered, kicking his ball high in the air then catching it neatly on his knee before it fell to ground.

He looked at the picture, and in just a few minutes he said in a broad local accent, "Yeah missus, I seen her."

Gus and I waited for him to continue telling us where she was, but he didn't, he started dribbling the ball around his feet, ignoring us.

"Well, where is she then?" Gus asked.

"Wots it worth?" the canny young Scot asked, still kicking his ball around.

Gus reached into his pocket, for his wallet and took out five pounds. He showed it to the young man., "Wow!" the boy said, looking straight at it. "It's real too!"

I didn't like to ask how many unreal fivers he'd seen or where they came from. The note held the boy totally absorbed, he looked at it with delight.

"It's yours if you tell us where she is," Gus prompted, half scowling, half smiling.

I'm not sure I like being outsmarted by such a young chap, but if it led to us finding Ellie, it would be worth it, I thought. At least with financial instincts like that he'll go far.

"She's away over there." He pointed towards some garages just short of the lorry park.

"What?" I screwed up my face in puzzlement. I was looking where he pointed but couldn't see anything that looked like it housed people. "But that's just garages."

"No. Not really. People live there," he said. "Me fiver now, Sir." Gus gave him the fiver, the boy shoved it quickly in his pocket and returned to kicking his ball.

For want of any better idea we walked towards the garages. You would never have guessed that people rather than cars were using the dilapidated buildings, but as we watched a figure vanished into a small side door.

"We'll go and knock there," Gus suggested.

"Ok," I replied. I couldn't think of a better plan. Thoughts of murdered children ran through my mind. I struggled to stop them.

As we approached I saw a frosted glass window crisscrossed with cracks and sporting a large gap. Through that I thought I could see a light. A very small light but a light nonetheless. I pointed it out to Gus, excited.

As we approached a woman came out of the little door. It rattled behind her on its hinges in the wind. The woman had long black shiny hair neatly plaited behind her and dressed in Indian style.

"Hi," I said showing the picture on my phone. "Have you seen this young woman?"

What if this lady wouldn't tell us where Ellie was? My stomach scrunched up with nerves as I tried to look as honest as I was.

She looked closely. Her gaze was scanning Gus and I as if quizzing our motives. She must have decided that we were all right.

"Yes." She replied eventually.

Opening of
BREAKER OF BONES
A historical novel by David Penny

Thomas Berrington came down to the river to wash, the ache in his bones reminding him of every one of his forty-two years. As he approached the water, sufficient light had gathered in the sky to show something floating and he stopped short. The water roiled slow and deep, stained offerings marring the surface. The object drifted from sight into a mist that obscured the river more than twenty feet from the bank. Thomas shook his head, convinced he had been mistaken. A second look at the water and he decided washing could wait until he entered Qurtuba.

He lifted his robe and pissed into the polluted river. Had it been cleaner he might have relieved himself elsewhere, but he didn't believe his own contribution was likely to make much of a difference.

His companions remained asleep. Pero beneath a blanket on the back of his cart, Jorge curled under his own blanket on the ground, his saddle for a pillow. It was almost the end of March but Thomas had discovered ice on his beard when he woke. He knew by noon he would be cursing his heavy cloak. They should have reached the city by now but Pero had insisted they take a detour two days earlier when rumour reached them of a skirmish near Castro del Rio. Now they were south of the Guadalquivir and still fifteen miles from their destination. The breadth and power of the river brought to mind the puny waters of his homeland of England, a place he hadn't seen since he'd left at the age of twelve.

Thomas was adjusting his robe when he heard something out on the water, the source hidden by the mist. He stepped closer to the bank but saw nothing as the sound came again. An oar dipping? A splash as something was dropped into the water?

Perhaps something moved, darker grey against grey, but he couldn't be sure and was reluctant to call out. Even this close to the city brigands might prey on the unwary.

Another splash was followed by two more. A shape pulled away upstream - it might've been a boat containing two figures, it might've been no more than a thickening of the fog. It slid in and out of the mist, never quite becoming visible as the sound of its passage faded. Thomas stared at the water as something drifted past and he took an involuntary step backwards. At first he took it for a child's limb, but then he made it out - the hindquarter of a wolf, the fur matted, the limb angled in a way to suggest it was not human. He watched it drift from sight, spinning slowly in the languid current. When he started to turn away, wondering why anyone would discard such a thing, another floated towards him. This time it caught against rushes beside the bank and Thomas, cursing the curiosity that had got him into trouble many times before, reached out with a stick and drew it close.

"What have you found now?"

He turned to see Jorge coming down the slope, picking his way delicately as if afraid he might tread in something unfortunate, which well he might. Even cold, unkempt and tired his friend still possessed the special aura that had picked him out to be a palace eunuch.

"Nothing."

"It looks like something to me." Jorge moved a few paces downstream to perform his own ablutions.

Thomas avoided looking, studying the severed limb instead. He turned it over with the end of the stick, leaned closer. A frown settled on his brow. Whatever he thought he had first seen it hadn't been this.

"Never seen a wolf's haunch before?" said Jorge, adjusting his robe as he approached.

"Why would anyone toss it into the river? An entire wolf, perhaps, but who would cut it up first?"

"Or torn apart." Jorge crouched beside Thomas, who knew his friend only pretended interest. They were closer now than before the business of last year which resulted in the ousting of one sultan and the ascent of another.

"So why throw it away? And see - this hasn't been hacked. The cut is clean, precise."

Jorge looked and shrugged. "As precise as you would be?"

"Perhaps not, but someone with skill did this."

"A butcher? I expect they have more practice than surgeons. Why should they not also be skilled?"

"They have no need of such precision. And a butcher wouldn't hack up a wolf."

"One more mystery in the world for you to solve," said Jorge, re-arranging his position so he could sit against the bank. "The priest is awake, by the way. He wants us moving. I told him I'd come and find you."

"You've found me."

"What are you going to do if you can't cure this prince?"

Thomas pushed the wolf's leg back into the current and watched it drift from sight. He thought the mist might be lifting a little. He could make out a rocky bluff on the northern bank, perched atop it some kind of fortified structure. "Go home," he said in response to Jorge's question, but the man had already disappeared and Thomas was alone again. He shook his head, both amused and frustrated at the eunuch.

Thomas rose to his feet, was starting to turn away when something else caught his attention, something different, paler, like the first sighting had been. He leaned over the water as the fickle mist chose to thicken at just the wrong moment.

The object drifted into the channel. Thomas took steps along the bank until it turned and approached closer once more. He looked around for another stick, found one, but whatever it was remained stubbornly out of reach. Even so he could make out what it was. This was no portion of a wolf. What he stared at was the headless torso of a young woman.

Tamara's emerald green eyes played with the screen as she opened Facebook, unable to resist the opportunity to check in with what was happening in the city she had left behind. She scrolled down the News Feed, giggling at her friend Beth's post showing a photo of her on a narrow boat travelling along the Norfolk Broads with her brother Heath. Beth was the skipper and she looked as though she were driving a car in the Grand Prix rather than a vessel that was moving slower than a push bike.

When Tamara left the UK for Australia, she didn't think she'd miss her drab flat with its tatty Formica kitchen floor and the slightly torn wallpaper beneath the lounge windowsill. She never imagined she'd miss the smell drifting up to her paper-thin windows every morning from the cafe across the road, or the sound of the twin toddlers upstairs wailing as their mother tried to get through the witching hour. But now, seeing such scenes with only the whirring sound of the computer for company, she yearned for that type of familiarity.

The leather chair creaked as she leaned into its backrest and smiled as she saw her message inbox receive a new mail. It was from Beth:

Really missing you, mate, but DO NOT COME HOME YET! (I'm writing this because I know you'll see

Facebook posts that make you feel as though you're missing out.
Believe me, you're not!)
Trust me; I've always had your back, haven't I? Ever since that Darren Wallis picked on you by the friendship tree. Blimey, wonder what he's up to now? God, who cares!
Anyway, gotta go. I've got an early meeting in the morning.
Say a big hello to the parents. Love and hugs!
Beth x

Tamara manoeuvred the mouse ready to reply, but her eyes jerked to the other side of the screen. She felt her body go cold as she froze, because there staring back at her was a Friend Request, from Bradley.

She wondered why she hadn't seen this one coming.

"Pah... I thought Facebook was for Losers!" She held her thumb and forefinger against her forehead in an 'L' shape, remembering how he had used those very words when she'd signed up to the social networking site. She realised then that she was rubbing her temple, and even though the bruise had healed pretty quickly, the memories still lingered of that night.

She shuddered as her mind flitted to Bradley's solemn confession about his family a couple of weeks into their relationship: "I hid under my bed like a coward," he'd said, as he described his father's rage. "I should've protected my mum."

The breeze from the open window made Tamara shiver now. She couldn't deny that she missed Bradley, and she wondered whether things could've been different if she'd made him get help, or if she had supported him more. The answer from Beth would be easy: a resounding "no"!

Sometimes Tamara fought to forget the good times so that she could open her eyes to the bad. Was that what she needed to do now?

Of course Bradley had a nice side, but not everyone got to see that. Sometimes he'd bought her flowers "just because"; he'd driven around for hours one night to get her flu tablets when she couldn't sleep and her temperature had gone through the roof; he'd cooked her breakfast in bed when she had the hangover to end all hangovers.

Bradley had kind eyes, a soft voice, and all the vulnerability of someone with a shaky past which Tamara had found herself responding to. Could she really push him away when he was reaching out to her, the girl he described as his "best friend"?

Two rectangular-boxed options waited on the screen for her to make her choice:

Ignore.

Confirm.

Her eyes looked first at one and then the other, unable to settle on either. She rubbed her hands against her bare legs, biting her lip as she refused to let her hands anywhere near the mouse. This was her chance; her chance to let him know that it was really time for them to go their separate ways.

Her hand returned to the mouse, moving it from side to side as though it were some kind of Ouija board:

Confirm, Ignore, Confirm, Ignore.
Click.

Opening of
HER SECRET ROSE
A historical novel by Orna Ross

What you need to understand is that they were like gods to us. Their height, for starters. This was a time when most of Ireland and England went half-hungry and a person was lucky to reach 5' 4" in his manhood. If you didn't see your ribs when you looked down at yourself naked, if you had a few decent rags to pull about your person, you were well got; if you'd two good meals a day and a winter coat, you were pure fortunate.

Then along would come those two, striding the full length of their legs down Grafton Street or Piccadilly. We'd stop and stare, even those who claimed to disdain them. Maud Gonne always wore a hat that added to her great height atop her Parisien finery, one of those concoctions they loved back then. Oftentimes too, they'd have the great dane stepping out in front of them, a slavering beast of a thing, tall as a donkey and as imperious as his mistress.

WB wasn't rich but he'd be costumed too. Every stitch, from the flowing tie to the black clerical cloak, from the eyeglass on a ribbon to the pointy black boots, chosen to announce the presence of a poet.

He was always delighted to be seen with her, that was the other thing you'd notice. Though he'd be stuck into whatever he was talking about, head bent, all intense, two hands fluttering like captured birds in front of his chest, still you could see that awareness sitting upon him: Look at me, walking down the highway with Maud Gonne.

Everything you've heard about her beauty is true. Never listen to those who say otherwise, they're being pure political. And don't mind the photographs, they don't do her justice. You had to be in her presence to experience it, to understand why it drew every man in the room, whether he was for the cause of Ireland or against.

Oh yes, they were a queer pair, Mr Yeats and Madame Gonne, Miss Maud and Master Willie. You may already have heard all sorts about them. Don't believe the half of it, the quarter of it, even. Much of it comes from the scholars and most of them are too intellectual, too protected in their choice of life, to understand what went on between those two wild, bewildered souls.

I saw it all for myself for I lived in Dublin and in London and in Paris too, in the last years of the old century, as did so many of we Irish in exile. I knew everyone who knew them.

Now there's near none of us else left of their generation or mine, and it's left to me to tell the truth of it all, before I'm gone m'self. For, bedazzled and distracted, the world has once again forgotten what it most needs to know.

We'll begin on January 3rd 1889, in Bedford Park in London, which the scholars - going on WB's word - accept as the where and when of the first meeting.

WB. Double-You-Be: that's what I call him. It has a nice pun to it, I think, for a man who was so divided on himself.

And didn't he write it up so nicely? How she came spinning in to the family abode and knocked them all -

especially him - sideways, with her great stature and her Valkyrie features and her luminous complexion and her bronze hair and, most of all, her passionate energy with its lacing of tragic vulnerability.

A combination guaranteed to lance straight to the heart - and nether regions - of a fin de siècle poet.

He was, as he always said, the last of the romantics and in the month Maud Gonne came calling, he'd just published a long poem full of mists and caverns and castles. And a hero compelled to gallop after an exotic seductress.

> A maid, on a swift brown steed
> Whose hooves the top of the surges grazed,
> Hurried away, and over her raised
> An apple of gold in her tossing hand;
> And following her at a headlong speed
> Was a beautiful youth from an unknown land.

Oh yes, he had himself well prepared for instant infatuation.

Maud Gonne always insisted they met earlier, at the house of John O'Leary, when WB was still an art student, in Dublin. O'Leary, one of the last of the old Fenians, was mentor to them both, to any young person of that time who took the cause of Irish freedom as their own. Willie had carried her books from Mr O'Leary's house to her hotel, Maud said.

She said, he said, they said...

Something you have to hold in your head as you read their sayings -- the poems or the letters, the books or the diaries -- is that there were two Maud Gonnes and two WB

Yeats: the living, breathing woman and man, what he called "the bundle of accident and incoherence that sits down to breakfast", and the creations they made to feed the newspapers and stalk the history books.

For him, the relationship started on the day she came calling to his father house in London and, like most everything that passed between them, his has become the accepted account. But me, I prefer to weigh male and female, outer and inner, public and private, in equal measure.

When looked at from the woman's side of the bed-sheet, most tales take a turning. And this one more than most.

So: London in the year of 1889, on the early afternoon of Wednesday, 30th of January. Here, buttoned and bonneted, comes Miss Maud Gonne, 22 years old, banging the hall door of her uncle's Belgravia home behind her, half-running down the pathway.

She's spent the morning chattering with her sister Kathleen and cousin May, who are always delighted when she whirls in from France with her animals and birds, holding out presents for all, her generosity and devil-maycare attitude giving the English aunts and uncles a shake-up. The young ladies have new beaus and a lot to discuss, so Maud finds herself, as usual, running late, pulling on her gloves as she goes.

The cab at the curb is a hansom, where the driver sits low in front, close to the horse. One of the new speedy ones, so she may yet be on time.

"Bedford Park, please," she says, sitting in.

The driver flicks the reins - "Right away, Miss" - and the horse begins its trot.

She picks up on the accent and leans forward to say, "You are Irish?"

"Indeed and I am."

"How very interesting. I have just returned from Ireland."

"Have you now? Whereabouts were you?"

"Co Donegal. Falcarragh. Do you know it?"

"I don't, Miss. But I hear tell it's beautiful in them parts."

"It ought to be. Alas, there is much distress."

Maud Gonne always liked to talk to cabbies or servants or peasants, those of us she called "The People". She thought us purer of heart than those of her own class and held that opinion all her life, through all evidence to the contrary. It was one of the reasons her Uncle William lately gave for saying she was not fit to be let out of the house.

But she is now of age, and Uncle William can no longer keep her locked down.

So she leans further forward to share the full drama of what she witnessed in Donegal: a woman who threw herself screaming up on the back of one of the bailiffs sent to evict her and her children clinging to each other by their rags, terrified of starvation or the workhouse.

"You're a rare one, Miss," the cabbie said. "A lady like yourself to care a bit about the like."

"I care a great deal, Mr...?"

"O'Driscoll, Miss. The Tipperary O'Driscolls. If you're ever in Borrisoleigh, you can enquire after the family. Just tell them Michael sent you and they'll organize anything for you. Anything you need doing. Anything at all."

He turns around and screws up his face at her in what she guesses is intended to be a smile. The conversation lapses, and Maud relaxes back. From Ebury Street, the journey takes them through the newly fashionable suburbs of Kensington, and then into the countryside and riverscapes around the new station of Hammersmith. Maud's mind is on what lies ahead.

For a time now, since her father died and she met her political ally, Lucien Millevoye, she has been collecting Irish nationalist contacts. That's what's brought her into this cab today, to taking this trip out to West London. She wants to meet the young poet who's making a name for himself, having recently issued two important, uniquely Irish books.

Mr O'Leary passed them to her and she read them with pleasure and admiration. Both affected her profoundly. The first is a book of folklore, tales of old Ireland she can't get out of her mind. The second, even more indelible, is a volume of poems called *The Wanderings of Oisin* (a Gaelic name pronounced, Mr O'Leary said, as Usheen).

The folklore is fascinating and strange, but the poems have lines so hauntingly beautiful and redolent of old Ireland that they have been circumambulating her mind since she read them, behind all her sleeping and eating and talking.

...[They]... came to the cairn-heaped grassy hill
Where passionate Maeve is stony still; And
found on the dove-grey edge of the sea A
pearl-pale, high-born lady.

A pearl-pale, high-born lady, who... rode... something. How did it go again? She couldn't quite remember now, but there were lines she knew she would never forget.

...Her eyes were soft as dewdrops hanging
Upon the grass-blades' bending tips
And like a sunset were her lips
A stormy sunset o'oer doomed ships...

She thinks he might have genius. Mr O'Leary believes so and his sister, Ellen has organized for her a letter of introduction to Mr John B Yeats, their friend, the poet's father. A portrait painter and, they say, quite bohemian, full of Irish conviviality. There are three younger offspring, two sisters and a brother: Lily and Lolly and Jack.

Everywhere, the Yeats family is spoken of as a slip of old Ireland in the branches of the new London suburbs. A light of artistic dedication among the murk of materialism. Willie and Lily and Lolly and Jack. Such names! She is keen to meet them but, yes, she is nervous. That's why she's talking too much to the cabbie. Intellectuals always make her nervous, more than any other class of people.

She hopes the O'Leary recommendation will carry her, that they are not anti-female, or inclined to think her an English spy. One could never tell in advance who would be an ally. In Dublin, Mr Oldham, middle-aged and bluff, had seemed unpromising, yet he had loved taking her to the Contemporary Club and throwing open the door and booming: "Maud Gonne wants to meet John O'Leary. I thought you'd all like to meet Maud Gonne."

With the Yeats family, she would do as she had done that day, when she'd felt so very shy. Mustering her courage, she had said, "Mr O'Leary, I have heard so much about you. You are a leader of revolutionary Ireland, and I want to work for Ireland. Can you show me how?"

He'd liked this direct talk; the frown had vanished from his ancient, cagey eyes, and he led her to a sofa, while Mr Oldham busied himself, making a cup of tea for them all.

"You must read," he'd told her. "Read the history of our country, I shall make you a list and lend you books."

A citron color gloomed in her hair
But down to her feet white vesture flowed, And
with the glimmering crimson glowed...

The clip-clop, clip-clop of the horse's hooves beat the rhythm of the beautiful, romance-soaked lines.

...And it was bound with a pearl-pale
shell That waved like the summer
streams, As her soft bosom rose and
fell...

It must be marvellous to be able to express one's feelings in words like that. She sits back into them, closes her eyes to the dullness of the grey expanse of London through which they pass.

In 1889, London is no longer the city made famous by Dickens, where rich and poor, healthy and afflicted, comingled public and private life on thronged and tiny streets. Now the centre and the east side teem with the underfed and under-clothed poor, while the middle classes expand the city out north and west. Roads upon roads of housing are being laid in long strips along the river and the passenger railways. Maud fancies if she were to take flight up out of the carriage and look down, she would actually see London ravenously advancing over the fields, its concrete army of houses felling hedges and trees, curling in around farms and fields, gobbling up villages and towns.

If she did, from that vantage she'd see up ahead, among the rows of grey, a warm cluster of houses built in what we now commonly called "London brick" but which was, back then, far more uncommon. Its color offered late Victorian Londoners the same pleasure as the scarlet petticoat of an Irish colleen: all the more pleasurable for being unexpected. This red-brick enclave is Bedford Park, where the Yeats family lives.

Uncommon too is the varied detail on each house, for Bedford Park is not inhabited by bowler-hatted Mr Pooters, swinging their brollies towards the 8.15, content to be one of many. It is home, in the main, to artists, writers and academics who prize individuality.

Now Maud's hansom cab pulls up in front of No 3 Bleinham Road. She lingers a moment to take a good look. A quiet and tree lined road; an attractive house appears roomy, with Dutch gables, white casement windows and a porch with decorative tiling.

"You can wait," she says to O'Driscoll. "I shouldn't be too long."

She knows she shall be at least an hour, but she would keep the fare running for his sake, so Mrs O'Driscoll and the little O'Driscolls, of whom there are doubtless a surfeit, might have a good week of it.

His profuse Irish thanks - "Thank you a million, Mam, and a million times more" - follow her out of the carriage, through the little gate, and up the pathway as she consciously pulls herself up, and steps towards the front door with what she hopes is calm dignity.

For a time, Maud Gonne had thought she might be an actress, had taken some training to annoy Uncle William and talked through many bedroom nights to her sister Kathleen about becoming a famous courtesan, consorting with the monarchs of Europe. She was young then and half-crazed in those days after dear Tommy had departed.

It was Millevoye, her Parisian friend, who had disabused her of this ambition.

"An actrice!" he'd snorted, in his French manner. "Pshaw! You underestimate your own power, my dear. An actrice, even one as great as Sarah Bernhardt, who is truly the greatest, even she only portrays the life of another. Where is the glory in that?"

They had agreed that instead she should make Ireland her stage. Now, on Ireland's behalf, she draws on her acting training to make her entrance. Suppressing a shiver, though it is not cold, not for January, she rings the doorbell with a sense of significance.

It is as if the bell is ringing down through the future, striking up the poetry that is to come, as if she knows in advance that the spiritual and political work she and the poet are to do together shall be a kind of poetry too. What she and WB create over the next decade will alter the history of two nations and will make them both famous, down through time. It is with just such an intention, vague and unclarified as yet, that she has come here today.

So when the serving girl answers the door, she speaks to her slowly, with a sense of import.

"I am Miss Gonne," she says, proffering her letter of introduction. "Miss Maud Gonne, lately come from Ireland."

A RAMBLING FANCY:
IN THE FOOTSTEPS
OF JANE AUSTEN
A travel memoir by Caroline Sanderson

I stayed the night in Bath in a beautiful Georgian guest house on the southern slopes of Bath, close to Beechen Cliff. My host and his partner welcomed me very warmly, invited me for a glass of red wine, and then for supper. The conversation turned to the eldest of my host's three teenagers, a boy of nineteen, whom, he felt, was a little too young to be getting so serious about his girlfriend. Though our lovely period surroundings had more than a whiff of Jane Austen's time, this was a dilemma of the modern era, light years away from a time when, at nineteen, many women were already married with children. Then we talked about marriage, and the difficulties of finding the right partner (my host was twice married and divorced) and how money – both a lack of it and a generous supply – has a tendency to complicate things. And suddenly we were right back in the 18th century.

Of course, women today have the luxury of being far more romantic about love and marriage than they did in Jane Austen's time. Then, most women – particularly those without independent means – were expected to take a pragmatic view of the estate, and get themselves off the shelf before their time ran out. Anne Elliot, still a spinster at the age of twenty-seven, has sacrificed a great deal by staying faithful to the only man she has ever loved, Captain

Wentworth. "Her attachment and regrets, had for a long time, clouded every enjoyment of youth; and an early loss of bloom and spirits had been their lasting effect."

Jane Austen also made a sacrifice. Not for the love of her life, but, I had begun to believe, for her work. In 1802, Jane left Bath with Cassandra on a visit to their childhood friends, Elizabeth, Alethea and Catherine Bigg at Manydown House near Basingstoke. During their stay, their younger brother, Harris, proposed to Jane. She accepted him, and the whole household went to bed, rejoicing at the match. The next morning, after a sleepless night, Jane decided she had made a mistake and declined his proposal. She and Cassandra left Manydown under a cloud and returned to Bath.

Harris Bigg-Wither was the heir to a considerable estate. Had she married him, Jane, at twenty-seven, would have been mistress of a large Hampshire house close to her birthplace, and could have assured the comfort of her parents and sister for the rest of their lives. This makes it more understandable perhaps that she succumbed to temptation, if only for one night. Of course she did not love Harris Bigg-Wither, but this was not an insurmountable hurdle. After all, another twenty-seven year old, Charlotte Lucas had embraced a worse fate in engaging herself to Mr Collins in *Pride & Prejudice* ("I am not romantic, you know. I never was. I ask only a comfortable home"). Surely what Jane Austen could not bear to give up was the freedom to write. For this, she was prepared to forsake what was probably her last chance of a suitable marriage. Let us give thanks for that sleepless night. As Claire Tomalin puts it in her biography of

Jane: "We would naturally rather have *Mansfield Park* and *Emma* than the Bigg-Wither baby Jane Austen might have given the world, and who would almost certainly have prevented her from writing any further books".

But what would Jane have done had she met a Captain Wentworth? Despite my very comfortable lodgings, I spent a disturbed night myself, notions of love and marriage and what they have to do with each other going round in my head until the early hours.

Jane Austen started writing a new novel whilst living in Bath. *The Watsons* – which sadly remained unfinished - puts the thorny subject of marriage under the spotlight as never before. Jane Austen began it in 1803 or 1804, not long after she had turned down Harris Bigg-Wither. When the novel opens, its heroine Emma Watson has just returned to the bosom of her genteel but poor birth family after many years away, during which time she has been brought up by a wealthy aunt. The aunt has remarried, depriving Emma of the generous inheritance she might once have hoped to have. Emma's rediscovered sister Elizabeth speaks movingly of her desperate need to find a husband: "You know we must marry. I could do very well single for my own part - a little company and a pleasant ball now and then, would be enough for me, if one could be young forever, but my father cannot provide for us, and it is very bad to grow old and be poor and laughed at".

The chequered business of finding and marrying the right man is something that all Jane Austen's novels have in common. Jane sympathises with Elizabeth Watson when in her plight she concludes: "I think I could like any good humoured man with a comfortable income". But as she lay awake after accepting Harris Bigg-Wither's proposal, the thoughts going round and round Jane Austen's head were surely closer to those of Emma Watson, who declares: "Poverty is a great evil, but to a woman of education and feeling it ought not, it cannot be the greatest". Romantic? Not very.

Extract from Chapter 1 of
UNRAVELLING
A novel by Lindsay Stanberry-Flynn

There should be a scar. Vanessa's often imagined it, an ugly, angry weal crawling over his forehead. Her eyes search for it. The wall light above his head creates a pool of shadow, and she can't see it. His head is cocked at an angle, just as it used to be, as if the rest of the world's out of kilter with him and he's trying to make sense of it.

She steels herself for the moment he'll look up, but he's staring into the flickering glow of the candle on the table. The waiter turns to her and raises his eyebrows. He gestures to the table, but she shakes her head.

She edges away. Retreats. Back through the long room, past tables with their white linen cloths. People. A couple, heads close. His fingers trailing through her blonde hair. Her lips lifting in a smile. A group. The flash of raised glasses. Mouths open ... laughter. She can't hear it. The thrumming in her ears drowns everything out. Her gaze flits over the wood-panelled walls, up to the chandeliers. Like spiders, waiting. The scent of the lilies on the mahogany dresser inside the door catches in her throat.

At last, the hotel foyer. The grandfather clock next to the reception desk chimes seven. Her heart races against its steady beat.

The maitre d' appears at her side. 'Is everything all right, Madam?'

'It was hot in there.'

'Would you like some water?'

She shakes her head.

'Shall I call your guest to come?'

His questions circle like a persistent bluebottle.

'If you could give me a minute?'

'Of course, Madam. You can sit here.' He indicates a low leather sofa. 'I'll tell your guest you'll be with him shortly.'

She perches on the edge of the sofa. Her velvet trousers cling to her thighs and her wooden beads feel tight at her throat. It's not too late to escape. She glances up at the staircase, imagining the smooth wood of the balustrade cooling her palm. The tranquillity of the hotel room will calm her. With its view over the leafy square, it's the one she always asks for when she stays in London. Her clothes hang in the wardrobe; her make up is scattered on the bathroom shelf; her laptop is on the desk. The items are familiar, part of the pattern of her days. She can phone down to reception, ask them to tell him she's unwell. She imagines his face as he listens to the waiter's whispered message. He's bound to be disappointed. 'I can't wait to see you again,' he said in their last phone call. She remembers the deep creases that made his heavy brows merge when he was cross or disappointed, the pouting lower lip, the way he would drag his hand through his already unruly hair.

His hair. Black, wild, gloriously wild. But not now. She sees again the shorn head, pale and vulnerable, bending towards the candle on the table. Shorn. Shriven. Forgiven. Not now. Not yet.

The years have left their mark on her too. She fingers her eyes where she knows he'll see a network of lines that weren't there when he last saw her. The furrows on her forehead that gathered permanently after the accident. But her hair is still much the same: a golden red that he liked to call titian; curly, always escaping from the comb she tries to tame it with. And her body is slim. True, her breasts have grown heavier and fuller, and the ice-sharp hip bones that he used to complain dug into him in bed are now covered with soft flesh.

The maitre d' reappears. 'Is Madam ready now?'

She stands up. An invisible hand seems to propel her forward, compels her to place one foot in front of the other. Her heels click on the marble tiles. They reach the heavy oak doors, and the maitre d' looks back, as if he's checking she's still there.

'If you'd like to come this way.'

They pass through the tables with their white linen cloths. They'll be there in seconds. No time to calm her breathing, reorganise her face into a sleek smile.

He doesn't seem to have moved in the time she's been away. His gaze is still fixed on the flickering candle, as if it might go out if he doesn't keep watch.

He glances up and gets to his feet. He's wearing a tweed jacket. What has happened to him that he wears tweed jackets? He holds out both hands and she notices how bony his wrists are. He smiles. It's a lop-sided grin with none of his old arrogance. But where's the scar? There should be a scar. He puts his arms round her and she breathes in, expecting to smell cigars. Instead she gets an aroma of expensive after-shave. He used to hate after-shave.

'Vanessa,' he says. 'Beautiful butterfly.'

She draws back from the embrace. 'Hello.'

He laughs. That same billowing laugh. The laugh that makes you want to fling your arms in the air and dance. 'What's so funny?' she asks.

He shakes his head. 'I've imagined this so many times. How it would be. What you would say.' He laughs again, this time a little puff of sound that has a world of hurt in it. 'And all I get is hello.'

She finds it then. The scar. It's absorbed into the wrinkles on his brow, a fine line faded to silver.

As they sit down, he covers her hand with his, and she sees he's wearing the signet ring she gave him on their wedding day.

Extract from
SHADOWS OF THE LOST CHILD
A historical novel by Ellie Stevenson

Late nineteenth century – Thomas

I'd thought Alice was just like us, like me and Louise. Well, not like us, she was different, posh, but a kid all the same, who liked to laugh when things went right and ended up sad when things went wrong. But Alice was something else entirely.

She'd pulled the square thing out of her bag and I saw up close that it wasn't really square, but more rectangular. She pressed her thumb to the front, gently, the part she told me was called a screen, and the thing lit up with tiny pictures. On a blue background. She pressed again on one of the shapes and then there were letters, like on a typewriter. I knew about typewriters because Miranda told me they had them at Chaucer's; she'd always wanted to work in their office. I told my mother, and she said the same, 'It's bound to be better than working in a laundry.'

My da had just laughed. 'You've got to be joking, you've no chance of that.'

Alice leant forward and touched the letters, one at a time, and words appeared in the space above them. 'Hi, I'm Alice.'

I was stunned, speechless. I couldn't think of a thing to say. I took a deep breath.

'Hello Alice, how are you doing?' She shook her head.

'Not like that, like this, stupid.' She grabbed my finger and at first I resisted, but she kept on tugging, and as I watched she guided my finger across the screen. I spelt out my name.

'Tom, to Alice.' 'Cool,' she replied.

'No,' I said, 'it's mild today.' Then Alice laughed, a genuine laugh, it was light and high and strong, from the heart. I realised then what had been missing, she'd looked very sad. But she wasn't sad now.

'No, cool, it means, good, okay, I approve, not cool as in cold.'

'Fine. If you say so,' I said, thinking, Really? How daft, but, of course, I was pleased she was talking to me. Sort of talking, anyway. She was writing again.

'Here, you take it, you have a go.' She passed me the thing and I stood there frozen, afraid I might drop it. 'Go on, try it, it's called a tablet.' Now, I was confused.

'A tablet is something you take when you're ill.'

'It's also a computer, a flat computer. This one's an iPad.'

'What's an iPad, or a computer?' I felt bewildered. Alice wasn't posh, she was out of my league. I realised I was still holding the tablet. I put my thumb to the top of the screen and dozens of pictures appeared before me, all in colour. Which was weird, amazing. They were faces, people, and one of the people looked like Alice. With a small dark woman.

'Is that your ma?'

'Yes, that's my Mum. Her name's Cressida.'

'You don't look anything like each other. Do you take after your father, then?'

'Yeah, a bit, but my father's dead.'

'Sorry,' I said. 'Mine is too.'

She smiled again, a bond had been forged. She leant across me and typed once more.

'Can I take your picture, Tom?'

'Draw it, you mean?'

'No, silly. Take a photo, with this.' She rattled the tablet.

'What, now?'

'Yeah, why not?'

I looked around. I couldn't see anyone else about. It was getting late, the kids had gone home and so should I, and the streets were getting much darker now. I wasn't talking about the light. When darkness fell in Curdizan High, the shady types came out of the shadows. I stared at Alice.

The iPad must be a camera, I thought. I'd never met anyone else with a camera. I'd heard about photos and someone I'd known had a portrait done, but that had been for a special occasion. I shrugged, curious.

She took the tablet out of my hand, and quickly held it in front of her face. I saw a flash.

'Not bad,' she typed. 'But wait a minute, where are you?' She pushed it across and pointed, carefully. I peered at the screen.

The view was there, just as I saw it, the gate, the back of my school by the churchyard, and in colour, that alone was enough to amaze me. But I was missing. I had been there, waiting and wondering what she would do, I'd seen the flash, and then I'd wanted to see the photo. But I wasn't in it.

'No,' I said, 'that can't be right.' The picture first, there straight away, and in colour, and me not in it. It was all too much. I looked at Alice and backed away. This girl was different and I was afraid.

I turned around and ran like hell, down the road and off to the right, through the alley, squeezing past some huddled bodies. I only slowed my pace at Croston. I kept on walking, heart beating fast until I reached Haversham Road and home. It really felt like home for once.

Extract from
WHITE MOUNTAIN
A fantasy novel by Sophie E Tallis

The midday sun passed into a hazy afternoon. The last soldiers descended, and the host were on their way again, marching at a great pace to recover lost time. The landscape changed around them. Flat plains and rambling hills of tussock gave way to gnarled weather-beaten rock and thicket beds, their needle like thorns starkly black against the grey granite.

The ground sloped steadily downward before levelling, where the barren expanses of rock fell away into mud, reed and bog. They had reached the Shudras, the silent marshes.

Slimy quagmires stretched out before them as an endless sea. Troughs of stagnant water riddled their way into hazardous deep pools. Foul smelling vapours rose from the ground in choking clouds. The thought of crossing such a place lowered all their spirits.

Following Korrun and Hallm, the army began their arduous crossing.

It was well into the night before the last exhausted traveller reached the delights of hard ground once more. They set up camp, the slimy mud and stench of the marshes clinging to each bedraggled member as an unwelcome reminder of the day. A deep unease fell on them.

Korrun sat quietly by one of the campfires, listening to Lord Tollam and Hallm speculate, in hushed tones on the battle to come.

"It could be a Hal'Torren's choice all over again," Hallm commented.

The other dworlls nodded grimly.

"Hal'Torren's choice? What's that?" Korrun asked.

Hallm shrugged. "It's any situation where the outcome is predetermined or unavoidable, and usually terrible."

Lord Tollam poked the fire, his violet eyes reflecting the glimmer of the flames. "It is an old legend, but a true story. Hal'Torren was a nobleman, strong, incorruptible, a hero and leader to his people. He lived in Oralam, a beautiful city once. One day he returned home to find his family held hostage by his sworn enemy, M'Sorreck. Hal'Torren loved his family deeply, his wife, his three young children. He offered his life in exchange for theirs. But Morreck wanted something far more precious. He wanted to break Hal'Torren utterly." Tollam sighed. "No matter what he did, how he bartered and begged, Hal'Torren was given a dreadful choice. Watch ten thousand of his own people perish, innocent children and families like his own, to save just one member of his family, or save his people and watch all his family die. Now Hal'Torren was a great leader, and he loved his people, but like any father, how could he sacrifice his own family?"

Korrun looked at the wise old dworll. "What did he choose?"

"To condemn ten thousand souls to a grisly death, to save one of his family." He shook his head. "Then he had to make the worst choice of all...which member of his family to save. That is Hal'Torren's choice. It is no choice at all. You are damned whichever path you take!"

"How did it end?" the dwelf asked quietly.

Lord Tollam sighed and glanced at his son as if thanking the gods that he never had to face such a choice. "Tragically of course...he chose to save his daughter, the youngest of his three children. They were then forced to watch his wife and two sons being murdered before them. Naturally, it traumatised the young girl. Only a few years later her father found her hanging from a willow tree. He promptly hung himself beside her. You see why Hal'Torren's choice is impossible. Save one, sacrifice others, condemn yourself."

"Morreck is a fengal beast, a monster!" Korrun said through gritted teeth.

"Yes, of the worst kind..." replied Tollam.

Hallm looked at his father for a moment then turned to the dwelf. "Have you ever faced a Hal'Torren's choice?" he asked.

Korrun shifted uneasily, his face half hidden in shadow. "Once," he whispered.

"What happened?" Hallm asked, trying to hide his surprise.

The dwelf stood up, his eyes lost in the fire. "I made the wrong choice," he said simply, then turned and left.

Extract from Chapter One of
TIME OUT OF MIND
A novel by Shirley Wright

I slide the desk drawer out for another quick fix. There it is – Penmaris, sitting four-square in the middle of fields, with nothing else in sight. Almost the air changes and I can breathe. I gulp down the whisper of a summer breeze, peer closer at the photo. You can tell the front door's open; I imagine that Paula has just walked through it with her camera to take this very shot from the end of the drive, framing the cottage in the landscape so it appears to rise naturally from rough grass and ancient stone. Since acquiring the snap a few days ago – "Here, Rose, have this one, it's recent. Nice sunny day in July. Be a bit nippy this time of year, though" – I have become obsessed with a tiny holiday cottage in the middle of nowhere. A place I've never visited, never seen, yet it haunts me like a melody I can't quite catch.

In the office I'm unable to focus on deadlines or art work and at home I cringe, suddenly overwhelmed by space. Our Clapham Common terrace has morphed into a cavernous sprawl I find intimidating. Instead, I pretend I'm living in this country cot, moving through its diminutive rooms, strolling the quiet garden to pick flowers, descending steep cliffs to the seashore to sketch the view: rock formations, a perfect seagull, waves breaking over shingle.

And always I am alone. Completely alone. Which is fine, because that's how it feels right now. After Peanut and the ghosts in his wake.

Dear God. Six months on, and I'm still assigning gender based on instinct. I bite my lip. Focus on breathing. The fact is, we'll never know.

Somewhere in the open-plan office a phone rings. I drink coffee and try to appear busy. One more peek at the photo and I promise myself I'll shut the drawer and get on with the Hansen contract. But this time when I glance at it, the picture seems different. A shadow lies over Penmaris and – how odd, I've not noticed that before – at the upstairs window, what looks like a face, someone's head and shoulders...

"Hi, Rose. What's up? Got your note."

My arm jerks, coffee spills. "Shit. You made me jump." I slam the mug down.

"Sorry. You okay?" Ellie drags a chair over to my desk and sits close. Her knees bump the drawer. "So, what can I do you for?"

The jokey manner disarms me, threatens my resolve. It's embarrassing to let her down. No, worse than that. I hate people who take advantage of friendship, and here I am about to exploit hers. Again.

"Well, actually, I'm thinking about... I know it's going to be a nuisance, but..."

Words skitter like autumn leaves. Ellie places a hand over the tangle of my fingers. "Stop picking, Rose. You'll make them bleed." She rummages in the open drawer and throws me the tube of hand cream. Then she sees the photo. "Pretty house. Where's this?"

I grab the snap from her, dismayed to find it splashed with coffee. What I had seen as a face at the window is now a blob of disintegrating celluloid. But the small disaster restores my voice. "I'm toying with the idea of going away, Els. Just for a while. Down to Cornwall. Next week, maybe, or the week after? Paula's said I can..."

"Paul?"

"Paula. And Chris. Our next-door neighbours?" Ellie nods. "They've said I can stay at their cottage. They don't get many bookings in October, so they're happy for me to... I need to be on my own, you see. I... I need to pull myself together, else I'll fall apart again."

People have hammered me with that phrase: pull yourself together – as if a broken puppet can repair its own strings. And I have tried – I've gone through the motions, knotting frayed ends with numb fingertips. But I feel like Pinocchio and I suspect my nose is getting longer.

Ellie is already tapping on her BlackBerry. "How does Oliver feel about this?"

"He can't possibly take time off, he's up to his eyebrows in work." Someone else I'll be dumping on, which is another reason why I'm hesitant. But Oliver's a workaholic, so he'll get by. I should be grateful he has a place to bury grief.

After punching a few more keys Ellie says, "All sorted. Viv can finish the Trueform job. Ah, what about Hansen?" A pause. More key punching. "Okay. Also sorted. Just give me a bell when you've decided."

I want to thank her but she cuts me short. "What are friends for, Rose? It's all right. I understand. Send me a postcard."

A short story from the collection
Quick Change

FUNERAL MARCH
by Debbie Young

For 17 years, Arnold Watson at 22 Kellaway Street and Derek Baker at number 26 had feuded over every neighbourly issue imaginable, from noise to parking to the clashing colours that they'd painted their front doors (one of them on purpose). Uncomfortably sandwiched at 24 was Clarrie Martin.

Clarrie was therefore surprised to notice Arnold creep in quietly at the back of the church, just before Derek was due to arrive by coffin.

A moment later, the *Funeral March* struck up, tremulous, on the church organ. Goodness, it was a while since she'd heard that played at a funeral, thought Clarrie. While she'd hardly expected Derek to plump for *Look on the Bright Side*, so popular at funerals these days, she'd rather expected to hear the opening bars of *My Way*.

Or perhaps the *Funeral March* was the default if you didn't specify otherwise? she wondered, like the chirpy ringtone that you get already set up on a new mobile phone. Clarrie tapped one brogued foot slowly in appreciation of the sombre rhythm.

She'd really felt rather more like dancing in this last week since Derek had passed away. It was like a weight had been lifted from her shoulders – or rather, her eardrums. Now that she no longer spent so much time with her hands over her ears muffling his shouting, her knitting was coming along so much faster.

The doctor said that Derek's death had been unexpected. Clarrie knew better. Watching his coffin progress slowly up the aisle on the shoulders of strangers, she speculated that Arnold failing to take in his recycling bin might count as the primary cause of Derek's death. He got almost as aereated over the binmen's schedule as Arnold did over Clarrie's cat digging up his garden.

Turning to leave the church after the ceremony, Clarrie sidled up to Arnold, her sensible shoes crumpling the fake rose petals still left lying on the ground since an earlier wedding. Ready to exchange the usual few hushed words in her special funeral voice, she was gratified to see that Arnold had been crying. Unclipping the gilt clasp of her shiny black funeral handbag, she drew out a floral scented tissue to offer him.

"There, there," she tremored, almost inaudibly. "I didn't realise you were so fond of poor Derek."

Arnold's whole body jolted, as if God had just flung him a small warning bolt of lightning.

"Fond? FOND? What makes you think I was FOND?"

His words bounced off the ceiling of the near-empty church. Arnold didn't have a funeral voice.

"It just upsets me to think that one day it'll be ME up there in a wooden box. Bloody Derek, always had to have the last word!"

Clarrie stared.

"And by the way, Miss Martin, it's about time you trimmed your front hedge!"

Turning his back abruptly, Arnold marched off towards his car, elbowing the vicar out of his way, who was standing in the church porch, hand outstretched for postfuneral shaking purposes.

On the bus ten minutes later, Clarrie made a mental note to replace the shrinking pack of tissues when she got home. It was always good to keep your funeral handbag well stocked, she thought, brightening. You never knew when you might need it next. She'd better put the cat out too.

THE BLACK TAIL OF CHAN -
A VERY SPECIAL CAT
(as told to Chris and Ann Dunn)

While the books sampled in the previous pages were published prior to the Festival, we were also pleased to launch on the night this affectionate autobiography by Chris and Ann's much-loved and much-missed pet cat, Chan. It's a sweet, easy-to-read book that will be enjoyed by adults and children alike. Here are the opening chapters:

My First Meeting with Dad and Mum

From the day we met, I called them Dad and Mum, and that's how I thought of them too. You see, I'd never known my real parents.

Apparently, when I was still very small, I was picked up wandering the streets of Gloucester, put into a cage, and carted off in some vehicle to a place where there were lots of other cats (and dogs).

One day, one of the helpers at this place took me out of my cage, and I made a real fuss of her, purring and trying to roll onto my back along her arm.

Then Dad and Mum were there, tickling my chin and generally making a fuss of me. Boy, did they seem keen! Somehow I knew straight away that we were going to be very happy together.

But then they were gone.

Going to my New Home

The next thing I remember is waking up with some tenderness around my groin and a general feeling that something was missing.

But what joy! Who should appear again but Dad and Mum? This time they were carrying some sort of cage.

Pleased as I was to see them, my enjoyment was tempered when they brusquely put me into the cage with another cat. This little tortoiseshell creature was quite sweet, but didn't really smell all there. It seemed she was coming with us.

Again we were put into a vehicle, much quieter than the one I had experienced before, but neither my companion nor I were very comfortable. We were cramped in that cage and kept being tossed about.

We weren't in there for long before Dad pulled the car up a steep but short road. We stopped moving, and everything went quiet, except for us.

A MESSAGE FROM READATHON
The children's reading charity

While the first Hawkesbury Upton Literature Festival focused on books for grown-ups, we recognise that a love of reading starts in early childhood, as highlighted by Orna Ross's poem Halo *at the start of this anthology. We therefore invited Vicky Pember, a Hawkesbury resident who works for the national charity Readathon, to tell us more about the wonderful work it does to spread the benefits of books and a love of reading among children and young people. This is the transcript of her presentation.*

Hello everyone. I'm here to tell you about work for Readathon, a charity that does two wonderful things. It helps children to love reading and supports seriously ill children at the same time. We do this through our two projects Readathon in schools and hospitals.

Now, imagine you are a child in hospital – you are lying in your hospital bed, you've been there for weeks now – you are desperately homesick, missing your own bed, your friends, even school and the familiar surroundings of home. Hospital is hot, it's noisy, beeping screens everywhere, some children are crying, adults around you looking exhausted and anxious, including your own parents - you feel guilty about that. You are in pain, people poke and prod you, you have no control over anything. The days are interminably long, nights longer and you feel utterly miserable. And then, around the corner, comes a bright orange bookcase filled with beautiful books. It's brought right up to your bedside. You choose a book from the wonderful selection and suddenly you are transported to another world - to a land of adventure away from the noises, smells and sights of the hospital – Mum starts to read with you too and you snuggle up and get lost in the story together. Because it's a brand new book you don't have to worry about more infections. Best of all the hospital teacher says you can keep the book forever.

Soon after a smiley man in a Readathon t shirt comes along; he's a storyteller and asks you what sort of stories you like. He creates tales of a bear and a magic gardener and before you know it you and Mum are both laughing your socks off - what a relief.

This is what Readathon does – in hospitals all across the UK. Every six weeks we fill the mobile Readathon bookcase with 120 brand new books and we provide regular visits from professional storytellers. No-one else does this. We make a difference to the way children (and their brothers and sisters,) in hospital feel – we cheer them up and take their minds off their worries which makes parents feel better too. Because of our Readathon books, these children tell us that they plan to read more when they leave hospital – that's the icing on the cake.

Readathon is in 26 hospitals across the UK and will reach 30 by August. We'll buy 25,000 books this year reaching over 100,000 hospitalised children in the UK. It's a fantastic project loved by everyone which is why we have the support of many publishers and authors like Malorie Blackman, Cressida Cowell, David Almond, Henry Winkler and Tony Robinson.

Now, down the road from the hospital is a school. There's a lad called Jamie there who loves school, but hasn't really got into a habit of reading despite much encouragement. One day, his teacher brings in a bright orange box and sets a challenge - to read as much as they possibly can, choosing whatever in the world they want to read, and get sponsored to do it. Well, Jamie loves a challenge, and when he hears it's to help other seriously ill children, he's really up for it. He'll read so that children in hospital can get lovely new books. Simple.

Readathon is the national sponsored reading event run by thousands of schools across the UK. It was started over 30 years ago by author Brough Girlin,g and you will all of course know Roald Dahl who was our first honorary chairman. You might have taken part in a Readathon yourself at school or sponsored your own children.

So how can you help? There are two ways you can help us – by directly donating here tonight or via our website (www.readathon.org) or text donate.

But there is something else that everyone in this room can do. It won't cost you a penny. It's easy and takes hardly any of your time. If you can encourage just one more school to run Readathon, then you will help us raise thousands of pounds. Once a school realises what a good tool Readathon is for getting pupils reading, they go onto to run it year after year. All you need to do is give the school one of our leaflets, direct them to the Readathon website and or call us and we will send them a free resource pack – they can run it at any time of the year. Tell us the name of the school you recruit and we'll let you know how they do. You could be kickstarting a life long love of reading.

As one Mum said when her son received a Readathon book "it couldn't have come at a better time – it turned tears into a smile". So please go out and recruit a new Readathon school or donate and you can put smile on a child's face today. Thank you.

Vicky Pember
Readathon Hospital Programme Director

We are pleased to announce that since our first Festival, one of our volunteers, Heidi Perry, has joined the organisation and is now working full-time doing wonderful work to spread the reach and impact of Readathon. She has also kindly agreed to be our Director of Children's Events - a new feature of the 2016 Hawkesbury Upton Literature Festival.

AFTERWORD

We hope you enjoyed reading this wonderful sampler, and that whether or not you attended the festival, you will want to read more by these authors. If you read any of their books in future, please consider leaving a short review on any online retail or social media site. Receiving a new review makes any author's day, as authors love to get direct feedback from their readers, and it helps new readers discover their work. Reviews of this anthology would also be very welcome.

And finally... we're hoping that connecting with so many published authors will inspire more members of our community to put pen to paper (or fingers to keyboard) themselves. On that note, we're ending this collection with Mari Howard's delightful poem about the lot of the aspiring author.

WANNABE...
A poem by Mari Howard

You know that wannabe thing?
*"But You're a **writer**! How **lovely** -*
I've always wanted
to write,"
she says ...

She smiles - all perfect teeth,
in her pashmina
and a little black number from Boden,
over purple leggings...

"And what do you do?" I say,
Defensive of my private imagination,
My Per Una evening wear
(last year's style)...
and guessing... *Lawyer, paediatrician,*
head-teacher,
market research? ...

*"But tell me about **you**,"* - she presses on,
"what do you write, and
would I have heard of you?"

I notice a change of personnel, a draught,
they have begun serving puddings in the
other room...
"Let's go through - after you," I say... (dropping back)

Writer? If the blood drains
from the chambers of the heart
best make it art -
form this shapeless river,
make letters, words,
tribute-eries to
experience ...
and, let's next time say, *housewife... mother ...*
cleaner and homework consultant?
Being a writer's romantic as
digging the allotment in war time,
And harder on the muscles of the back.

INVITATION TO THE 2016 HAWKESBURY UPTON LITERATURE FESTIVAL

Following the success of our inaugural evening event in April 2015, the Hawkesbury Upton Literature Festival will now be an annual event, held during the day-time to allow us to include more events and welcome more guests, and to expand from an adults-only festival into a family occasion. There will be a new Children's Festival, directed by Heidi Perry.

In 2016 it will take place once more on World Book Day which by chance will fall conveniently at the weekend, on Saturday 23rd April 2016.

For more information about the Festival all year round, please visit our website: *www.hulitfest.com*. Authors, poets or illustrators who would like to take part in the event are warmly invited to contact us.

In the meantime, happy reading!

Debbie Young Festival
Founder & Director

ABOUT THE AUTHORS

Ali Bacon

www.alibacon.com

Ali Bacon lives just down the road in South Gloucestershire. She is the proud mother of 2.4 novels and quite a few short stories, many of which have been published or won prizes. Her contemporary coming of age novel, *A Kettle of Fish*, was published in 2012, and two of her short stories are featured in *Unchained*, an anthology of fiction and poetry by local writers.

Jean Burnett

www.jeanburnett.com

Jean lives in Bristol. Her passions are books/writing/music/ cats and chocolate plus travel to out of the way places. She has a Master's degree from University Of Wales (Cardiff). Her books are *Who Needs Mr Darcy?*, published by Little, Brown (2012) in the USA as *The Bad Miss Bennet*, and *A Brazilian Affair: The Further Adventures of Lydia Bennet*, published by Matador as an ebook (2014). *Vagabond Shoes*, a travel memoir, is now available on Kindle. She has a short story in the *Unchained* anthology (Tangent Books) and short stories on the web. She is a former journalist and advertising copywriter.

William Fairney

www.dieselpublishing.co.uk

William Fairney is a Chartered Engineer with over 30 years experience in the Electricity Supply industry where he directed engineering and construction divisions in National Power. William was a Visiting Professor at Durham University for over 20 years and is founder and MD of FairDiesel Limited, a locally-based engineering company. Author of several books on biography and engineering, he is proprietor of Diesel Publishing and a member of the Bristol Books and Publishing group. He is also a Trustee of the Long John Silver Trust, whose aim is to promote the maritime and literary heritage of Bristol.

Katie Fforde

www.katiefforde.com

Katie Fforde lives in Gloucestershire with her husband and some of her three children. Recently her old hobbies of ironing and housework have given way to singing, Flamenco dancing and husky racing. She claims this keeps her fit.

J J Franklin

www.facebook.com/bren.littlewood

J J Franklin, aka Bren Littlewood, comes from a mental health and counselling background. She wrote scripts for the BBC before penning her first novel, *Urge to Kill*, a psychological thriller featuring DI Turrell, set in and around Stratford-upon-Avon where she runs a crime-writing group for the Bardstown Writers. The second book in the DI Turrell series is *Echoes of Justice*.

The Hawkesbury Writers

www.hawkesburyhistorybooks.wordpress.com

The Hawkesbury Writers is a group of villagers who, over the past 20 years, have produced three books under the title *A Monument to Hawkesbury*. These books have covered the changes in the village over the past 100 years seen through the eyes of those who have lived here. They are an aural and visual history of memories, anecdotes and photographs collected and collated up by the group. The group's editor is Jenny Harris who has been the driving force behind the project. The profits from the sale of the books has enabled them to donate thousands of pounds to village ventures and organisations.

John Holland

www.johnhollandwrites.com

John Holland is a short fiction writer from Stroud in Gloucestershire, and also the organiser of the twice yearly Stroud Short Stories event - see its website for more information: www.stroudshortstories.blogspot.co.uk.

Mari Howard

www.marihowardauthor.wordpress.com

Mari Howard (a pen name) is a city girl from London who's moved via Newcastle to live now (for many years) in Oxford. She studied social sciences and religion and now writes contemporary fiction questioning our present culture within the context of family-based novels (think Joanna Trollope and JoJo Moyes). Mari has three grown children and no grandkids, but three cats and a longsuffering husband, and enjoys baking and doing the garden as a foil to writing.

Christine Jordan

www.christinejordan.co.uk

Christine Jordan writes historical fiction set in Gloucester. Her debut novel, *City of Secrets*, was self-published in 2014. She is currently writing a non-fiction book for Amberley Press called *Secret Gloucester* which is to be published in October 2015. She is also researching and writing her second historical novel which is to be a trilogy based on the medieval Jewish community of Gloucester. She also writes children's books under the pseudonym of C J Gloucester.

Andrew Lowe

www.andrewlowewriter.com

Andrew is a writer, editor and journalist with absolutely no experience of book publishing. So he thought he'd better quit his job and get some. He's written for *The Guardian* and *Sunday Times*, and contributed to numerous books and magazines on film, music, TV, sex, videogames, and the treatment and prevention of sports injuries. He divides his time between various rooms of his home in London, where he writes and makes music (as half of electronic duo Redpoint). He gets out of the house by cycling and coaching youth football. *The Ghost* is his first novel, but it won't be his last.

John Lynch

www.jlynchblog.com

John Lynch is about to retire after 40 years in international sales, during which he never gave up the writing career that began when he was ten years old. He writes historical fiction (as R J Lynch) and (as John Lynch) contemporary fiction. Apart from a non-fiction book, *The International Sales Handbook*, John currently has three published books: *Zappa's Mam's a Slapper*, *Sharon Wright: Butterfly* and (set in the 1760s) *A Just and Upright Man*. A naturally gregarious person, he says isolation is the one thing he finds difficult about being a writer and he encourages readers to email him.

Michael MacMahon

www.michaelmacmahon.com

Michael MacMahon is a Bristol-based septuagenarian with no interest in retiring. Instead he's devoting his 'Third Age' to a portfolio career drawing on personal and professional experience, as an author, personal performance coach, speaker and voice actor. Read more about all of these activities at his website.

Rosalind Minett

www.characterfulwriter.com

Rosalind Minett (writing name) spent her working life as a chartered psychologist, her final 14 years as an expert witness. Predictably, the inner life of her characters determines their fate in her stories, whether humorous, historical or criminal. She relishes quirkiness, and creating complex characters whether these are in their prime, older or very very young. Rosalind avoids the expected author mugshot, using an avatar that looks nothing like her, Girl Before Word Processor (apologies to Picasso). The two faces suggest her serious and the irreverent selves. They also refer to the watcher and the seen, the inner and the outer person. She enjoys reviewing less usual work, such as translations of world fiction, but also reviews new authors. She is the author of *Me-Time Tales*: *tea breaks for mature women and curious men*, the trilogy, *A Relative Invasion* and the series, *Crime Shorts,* and has two psychological dramas in process.

P D Murphy

www.thelittlesummerofthequince.wordpress.com

Paul is a writer based in Bristol. His first book was published in June 2014. *As I Walked Out Through Spain in Search of Laurie Lee* is a tribute to the local writer Laurie Lee in his centenary year and deals with his Spanish Civil War years. Paul is currently writing a novella on Santa Teresa, the Spanish mystical poet of the sixteenth century in her 500th anniversary year and is researching a First World War creative non-fiction book set in Cardiff and the front line trenches based on his own family, a black sheep and a secret very much of its time. He blogs and writes for a range of publications including *The Guardian*, *The Huffington Post* and *Cotswold Life*. He is the secretary of the Bristol and South West ALLI branch of Independent writers.

Lynne Pardoe

www.lynnepardoe.com

Lynne worked as a social worker for 25 years before she retired due to ill health. "It's a job which is challenging, yet brings moments of great joy and reward. Where else could you help an abused youngster find a forever family, help a perpetrator learn new life skills, help a runaway teenager to a more settled future?" Now Lynne writes fiction based on her years in both child protection and mental health.

David Penny

www.david-penny.com

David Penny is the author of four science fiction novels and several short stories published during the 1970s. Near starvation led him down the slippery slope of work, which distracted him from his true calling. He has now returned to writing, and *The Red Hill*, a Moorish mystery thriller, was published in June 2014. The follow-up in the series, *Breaker of Bones*, was published April 2015.

Helen J Rolfe

www.helenjrolfe.com

Helen J Rolfe worked as an IT consultant until she couldn't ignore her passion for writing any longer. She studied journalism and writing and worked as a freelance journalist for women's magazines. She also volunteered as a media assistant with a not-for-profit agency where she was responsible for the corporate newsletter and media releases. In 2011 the fiction bug bit, and Helen has been writing fiction ever since. After fourteen years of calling Australia home, Helen has returned to the UK with her family and they now live in Bath. *The Friendship Tree* is Helen J Rolfe's debut novel.

Orna Ross

www.ornaross.com

Orna Ross writes novels, poems and the *Go Creative!* books, which are all about applying the creative process to life. She's Director of the Alliance of Independent Authors, work for which *The Bookseller* has named her "one of the 100 most influential people in publishing". Her latest project is *Her Secret Rose*, a special edition print book to celebrate #Yeats2015, the 150th birth anniversary of the Irish Nobel laureate poet.

Caroline Sanderson

www.twitter.com/CaroSanderson

Caroline Sanderson is a writer and books journalist. She is Associate Editor of *The Bookseller*, and editor of *ALCS News*, the monthly magazine of the Authors Licensing and Collecting Society. Caroline is the author of five non-fiction books including *A Rambling Fancy: In the Footsteps of Jane Austen*; *Kiss Chase and Conkers: the Games We Played*; and *Someone Like Adele*, a biography of the superstar singer. Her recent short biography, *Pocket Giants: Jane Austen*, was described by actress Emma Thompson as "a delicious acorn of a book... as spare, elegant and to-the-point as the literary oak it describes." Caroline is a regular broadcaster on radio. She is an accomplished public speaker, and also chairs events at literary festivals. She was a judge for the 2013 Costa Biography Award.

Lindsay Stanberry-Flynn

www.lindsaystanberryflynn.co.uk

Lindsay Stanberry-Flynn is an award-winning novelist and short story writer. Her novels, *Unravelling* and *The Piano Player's Son,* have been well reviewed, and many of her short stories have been published in anthologies and successful in competitions. Readers describe her novels as 'compelling', 'difficult to put down' with 'fantastic story and character development'. She also writes flash fiction, and set up the Worcestershire Lit Fest Flash Fiction competition for which she is one of the judges. Lindsay's third novel will be out later this year, and she combines writing with her work as a creative writing tutor.

Ellie Stevenson

www.elliestevenson.wordpress.com

Ellie has written two novels, *Ship of Haunts: the other Titanic story* and *Shadows of the Lost Child,* both partly historical with a dash of the supernatural and some ghosts. As well as exploring life on Titanic, *Ship of Haunts* examines the challenging world of the child migrant. *Shadows of the Lost Child* is a historical mystery with a time travel twist, set in a fictional city, inspired by historic York (UK). She has also written *Watching Charlotte Brontë Die: and other surreal stories.* Her writing is fuelled by inspiration, determination and plenty of coffee.

Sophie E Tallis

www.sophieetallis.wordpress.com

Sophie E Tallis was born in Bristol, UK, but grew up in a sleepy village just north of it, dreaming of dragons and wild adventures. She has subsequently travelled the world having many adventures but now lives in the Cotswolds with her family, two enormous white wolves, two even bigger Alaskan Malamutes and a load of wild ducks. She is a writer, poet, painter, artist and illustrator with a BA (Hons) Degree in Fine Art, photography and sculpture and a Post-Grad in Education, and is now a librarian, a dream job being surrounded by books all day! *White Mountain,* the first book of the *Darkling Chronicles* trilogy, was inspired by the author's experiences during a four month backpacking journey to New Zealand in 1997, an odyssey that changed her life.

Shirley Wright

www.facebook.com/shirley.wright.338658

Shirley Wright is a prize-winning poet and novelist from Bristol. Her short story *We'll Meet Again* won second prize in the Saturday Times competition for Halloween in 2008 and her novel *Time out of Mind* was published in 2012 by Thornberry Publications. It's a ghost story set in Cornwall. Shirley's poetry is widely published in magazines and journals, and her poem *My Father* won the *Telegraph* Poetry for Performance competition in 2008, judged by the then poet laureate, Sir Andrew Motion. Shirley's poetry collection *The Last Green Field* came out in 2013, published by Indigo Dreams.

Debbie Young

www.authordebbieyoung.com

Debbie Young has published two collections of short stories, *Quick Change* and *Stocking Fillers*, is writing a third, and is also working on her first novel. She also writes how-to books for authors and books about Type 1 diabetes. She is the editor of the Alliance of Independent Authors' advice blog, as well as being their UK ambassador. She is an avid reader, book reviewer and blogger. She writes regular columns for various magazines and is a member of the Hawkesbury Writers group. She appears frequently on BBC Radio Gloucestershire talking about books, writing and publishing. She speaks at events for writers and readers all over the country, but none is as close to her heart as the Hawkesbury Upton Literature Festival, of which she is founder.

ACKNOWLEDGEMENTS

First, huge thanks to all the contributors to this anthology, who gave their time voluntarily to take part in the first Hawkesbury Upton Literature Festival. I am extremely grateful to the audience who came along to support our new venture.

Many thanks to Aggie and Giuseppe at the Fox Inn for their hospitality, and to the team of volunteers who worked quietly and efficiently behind the scenes: Ali Bacon, Sara Couzens-Short, John Holland, Sara Musty, Heidi Perry and Caroline Sanderson.

Thanks also to my husband, Gordon Young, for his help and support from conception to execution; to our daughter Laura Young and her friend Nina Sorrentino for their help on the night. Thanks too to our friends Mike Easterbook and Helen Zukovsky for helping clear up the next day, for picking me up when I fell over on the way home, and for making me go to A&E the next day to treat a suspected broken elbow.

I'm looking forward to doing it all again next year, though preferably without the hospital trip!

Debbie Young